The One- Man Army

Cover design by Bill Toth

Book design by Iris Bass

Footprint courtesy of John Molish

Author photograph by Stephen Fischer

The One-Man Army

MOACYR SCLIAR

Translated by
Eloah F. Giacomelli

AVAILABLE
PRESS

BALLANTINE BOOKS • NEW YORK

An Available Press Book

Library of Congress Catalog Card Number: 85-91160

ISBN 0-345-32858-2

Manufactured in the United States of America

First Edition: January 1986

☆☆

1970

IN THIS SEA CAPTAIN BIROBIDJAN NOW LIES AFLOAT, motionless, half-drowned. From the wharf the little men watch him in silence.

Birobidjan strikes his hand into something hard: It's the keel of a boat. Immediately, he rallies and climbs aboard the small sailing vessel.

There is no one there. The captain begins making ready to sail. Someday he'll make a drawing of himself, showing him standing at the prow, his head held high, his searching eyes probing the darkness; someday, when he has time for the arts. Now there is so much to be done. He has to return, sail up the Guaíba Delta, dock at the harbor in Porto Alegre, and then go to Beco do Salso. There, at the place he once named New Birobidjan, he'll call his comrades to a meeting and will announce in a firm yet calm voice:

"At this moment we begin the building of a new society."

He must return. Mayer Guinzburg—Captain Birobidjan—hoists his flag up the mast and gets ready to sail.

*   *   *

They laid Mayer Guinzburg on a stretcher. A nurse wheeled him to the outpatient section, leaving him in the hall for a moment while she entered a room to talk to the attending physician.

"There's a patient outside ..."

She was cut short by a yell; they dashed out into the hall, where they found the man, his head thrown backward, his eyes staring wildly, his lips purple. Quickly the doctor listened to his heartbeat with the stethoscope, then shouted, "Cardiac arrest!" He tried to loosen the straps that tied the patient down; when he didn't succeed, he climbed onto the stretcher and started to massage the man's thorax. "What are you waiting there for?" he yelled at the nurse, who stood there motionless, frozen with fear. "Give me a hand. Try mouth-to-mouth resuscitation." She hesitated for a moment, then climbed onto the stretcher also, placed her lips against the man's limp mouth and started to blow furiously. Other nurses were rushing up to them. The doctor was shouting instructions: Bring in the anesthetist, set up the serum, hook up the defibrillator ...

Four or five people were now working on the lifeless body when all of a sudden the stretcher began to move. The doctor, losing his balance, fell to the floor. The stretcher disappeared at the end of the dark hall.

"Where is he going?"

"To New Birobidjan," shouts the captain. The little men cheer enthusiastically.

The captain puts the finishing touches to his preparations and will soon be ready to leave.

The tide will rise, the sail will swell out, the boat will leave. Captain Birobidjan will set sail.

☆☆☆☆☆☆☆☆☆☆☆☆☆☆☆☆☆☆☆☆☆☆☆☆☆☆☆☆☆☆☆☆☆☆☆☆☆☆☆

1928

One day Mayer Guinzburg entered a coffee shop in Bom Fim.

"Coffee, Rosa."

"Right away, Captain!" shouted the waitress, scalding a cup.

Mayer Guinzburg turned pale. Going behind the counter, he grabbed the woman by the apron.

"Don't you ever call me 'Captain' again, do you hear? I'm not a captain. I'm just a person like you, your equal."

"But ... what shall I call you then?" she stammered.

He hesitated before replying.

"Comrade. Call me comrade."

"Okay, Comrade Senhor Mayer."

"No. Comrade Mayer."

"Comrade Mayer."

"That's right. Or Comrade Mayer Guinzburg, if you prefer."

"Comrade Mayer Guinzburg."

"That's right. Now get me the coffee, will you."

"Captain!" somebody shouted in a deliberately high-pitched voice.

Mayer Guinzburg turned around abruptly. Seated at the tables, the Jewish tradesmen of Bom Fim* were smiling at him. Chagrined, Mayer Guinzburg turned to Rosa and asked for the sugar.

"Captain!" It was the same scoffing voice again. "Captain!" now someone else was shouting. "Captain! Captain!" The shouts came from all around. Mayer Guinzburg realized that from then on he would always be the Captain. "Captain! Captain!"

Birobidjan. In 1928 the Soviet government set aside ten million acres of land for the purpose of establishing an autonomous Jewish region in Birobidjan, in eastern Siberia.

There were several reasons behind this governmental decision, among them the need to set up a barrier against Japanese expansion. The government hoped that this undertaking would foster an economic substratum for the Jews in a region where they would also be able to develop their Yiddish culture.

It was hoped that thousands of collective farms would spring up there. Crops; livestock (especially chickens, goats, and even—and why not?—pigs, for at last religious superstitions would disappear); mills and factories; cultural institutions. All of this would transform the Jews—tradesmen, bureaucrats, intellectuals—into workmen. Mayer Guinzburg quivered with emotion when he discoursed on Birobidjan. People in Bom Fim laughed at him, calling him Captain Birobidjan, which enraged him, but his progressive stoicism kept him silent. To react would merely give his irreverent listeners further opportunity to taunt him. Besides,

---

* *A Brief history of the Jewish Tradesmen of Bom Fim.* During the first decade of this century, the Jewish Colonization Association, a philanthropic group sponsored by the wealthy Rothschild family, bought land in Rio Grande do Sul. Jews from eastern Europe (mostly from Russia), trying to escape from the pogroms, were brought as settlers. This enterprise, however, proved less than successful (due to the fact that it was a typically capitalistic venture, according to Mayer Guinzburg). The Jews left these settlements (Quatro Irmãos, Philipson, among others) for Porto Alegre and other cities and towns, where they became tradesmen. Some set up small stores that carried clothes and cheap furniture; others peddled clothes hangers, neckties, and so forth, or sold goods on the installment plan.

Mayer didn't want people to associate Birobidjan with flippant jokes.

Birobidjan. Someday the Jews in Bom Fim would recognize the importance of this name. Birobidjan would redeem the Jewish people and end their peregrinations. Birobidjan!

In 1928 Mayer Guinzburg was a lean young man, with glittering eyes and a wild mien. A self-portrait from that year depicts him wearing a cap on his disheveled hair, a gray scarf around his neck, a worn-out leather jacket, boots. His hand, outstretched, points to the road to be followed. The rising sun lights up the face of this leader. In the background, dozens of emaciated little men: the masses.

1928. Mayer Guinzburg, his girlfriend Léia, and his friend José Goldman would take walks in Redenção Park. It was cold but it didn't matter to them: They ran, leaped, rolled on the grass, laughed and sang.

Léia would recite poems by Walt Whitman.

> *"Pioneers! O pioneers!*
> *All the past we leave behind,*
> *We debouch upon a newer mightier world, varied world,*
> *Fresh and strong the world we seize, world of labor and*
> *the march,*
> *Pioneers! O pioneers!"*

Walt Whitman. After 1848 Walt Whitman began to seek out the company of workmen and lower-class people, Léia would explain. Up to then he used to dress like a dandy, but in that year he began to wear rustic clothes. He wanted to hug the people, to kiss the people, to blend himself into the people. As she recited, Léia quivered with emotion. A gentle woman with blond hair, Léia had lived alone with her father since she was five years old, when her mother deserted them. The father was in poor health, and whenever annoyed with Léia, he used to say that she would be the death of him, which made Léia cry very often. Then she would wipe her tears, get together with her friends, and recite poetry to them.

José Goldman would read from his "Song to Birobidjan":

"I am Birobidjan, a region blessed with rich soil and lush green forests. To ye, O Jewish workmen, I open my breast. Come! Put forth roots in me, teach me to quiver at the sound of your Jewish songs! Let your plows make furrows in my flesh, and I'll reward you with abundant crops. Come, O ye!"

Mayer Guinzburg, Léia, José Goldman. The three of them would talk about a great nation; about the peasants and workmen— tall men with bushy eyebrows, gloomy but proud eyes, broad chins. They would talk about the strong, silent women, with kerchiefs covering their heads, holding children in their laps. They would talk about hammers and saws, about tractors and combine harvesters. They would sit down and talk. They would get to their feet and start to walk, talking nonstop, and later they would be running and leaping about in the park, Mayer always leaping higher than the others to pluck leaves off the trees. If they saw a policeman, they would hide themselves; and hidden, they would whisper and laugh. In 1928.

Mayer Guinzburg is full of ideas. They'll start a collective farm—Léia, José Goldman and he. It will be located some distance from Porto Alegre, but not too distant, of course, because that's where the Great March will start someday. There will be a flagpole with the flag of New Birobidjan fluttering in the wind. They'll sow corn and beans. They'll treat the plants as friends, as allies supporting them in their undertaking. They'll raise a pig—Comrade Pig; a goat—Comrade Goat; a hen— Comrade Hen. Comrade Goldman will be fond of Comrade Pig, Comrade Léia will be fond of Comrade Goat, but Comrade Mayer Guinzburg will dislike Comrade Hen. He won't be able to explain why, but he'll dislike her. Although he'll try hard to like her, he won't succeed. Léia will criticize him; he'll own up to his error yet be unable to do anything to correct it. They'll live in huts, and the Palace of Culture will be located in a small lean-to. There the drawings of Comrade Guinzburg will be exhibited, and Comrade Léia will recite Walt Whitman, and Comrade José Goldman will read his proclamations. Will the settlement publish a newspaper? *The Voice of New Birobidjan,* edited by Comrade Mayer Guinzburg, will print manifestos, international news, and even a leisure section with crossword puzzles and news about chess games.

One night when he finds it impossible to sleep, Mayer Guinzburg writes in longhand an entire issue of the newspaper, which he also illustrates with various drawings. At dawn he decides to show the newspaper to his comrades. He runs down Rua Felipe Camarão, then turns into Rua Henrique Dias, where Léia and José Goldman live. The old Jews on their way to the synagogue eye him suspiciously, but he's not afraid of them; no, he isn't. He is dauntless.

Léia lives next door to the grocery store. Mayer Guinzburg taps on the window three times; she appears, smiles, signals to him, and a moment later is out in the street, shivering with cold. They walk toward a row of small wooden houses and stop at the one where José Goldman lives to wake him up.

The comrades approve of the newspaper, but José Goldman is critical of the chess. He dislikes games in general, particularly card games with their playing cards full of kings, queens, and knaves—a bourgeois vice. In his opinion, kings are fat and stupid; they eat a whole chicken, then belch, fall asleep and lie snoring; whereas queens, wicked, poison the wine of their enemies. As for knaves, well, they are responsible for all the plotting and scheming common in the courts. José Goldman has similar objections to chess. José Goldman: rather short, with red hair, myopic. High-strung: whenever he argues a case, he trembles and his voice breaks with emotion. Mayer, however, assures him that the Russians love chess; José Goldman is shocked to hear that, but in the end, although reluctantly, he agrees to the idea of having chess news in *The Voice of New Birobidjan.*

Deep in his heart he believes that someday the pawns will advance, not from square to square, but in giant strides, overthrowing kings, queens, bishops, knights; knocking down their horses and castles. People's tribunals will be established, the accused will confess, heads will roll. The chessboard will become the Republic of the Pawns. There won't be white and black squares anymore; all squares will be the same color and belong to everybody—if two pawns want to share the same square, they will be able to do so; if three want to share a square, they'll be able to; if four, likewise; if five, the same; if six, seven, twenty, they'll be able to. There will be room for everybody. In the Republic of the Pawns there will be houses, factories, farms, and the Palace of Culture will be housed in the king's old mansion. All of this yet to come.... Meanwhile, seated on the curb on Rua Henrique Dias, they read *The Voice of New Birobidjan,* trembling with cold. Old Sruli, Léia's father, walks past them on his way to the synagogue. He looks at his daughter with disgust, but says nothing. José Goldman stores the manuscript of the newspaper in his pocket and says good-bye. He has to go to work. Mayer and Léia, hand in hand, go for a walk in Redenção Park.

☆☆☆☆☆☆☆☆☆☆☆☆☆☆☆☆☆☆☆☆☆☆☆☆☆☆☆☆☆☆☆☆☆☆☆☆☆☆☆

1916

WE LEFT RUSSIA IN 1916 SAYS AVRAM GUINZ-
burg, Mayer's brother. We came by ship, and threw up a lot
... and yet, to the best of my recollection, we were happy. Yes,
happy. Father was sick and tired of Russia and ever since the
pogrom in Kishinev, Brazil had been constantly on his mind.
True, Russia was the homeland of Sholem Aleichem and of many
other great Jews, but to us it was hell. There was a storm on
the sea that lasted two days. We were seasick and cried, be-
moaning the sad fate of a wandering people and ... but the
sun shone again and we talked about Brazil. Leib Kirschblum
will do well in his business, we said, and indeed, he did well.
Avram Guinzburg will get married, they said, and have many
children, and indeed, I got married and had many children.

Mayer would hardly say a word to any of us. Silent, he would
sit at the stern, gazing at the sea. He was thinking of Russia,
imagining that in October, 1917, a revolution would take place
there, aimed at freeing the poor and the downtrodden. He imag-
ined that they would write about him in a newspaper called
Pravda:

The departure of Mayer Guinzburg is a great
loss to Russia, where we had an important place
for him. Yet, never mind! We know that Mayer
Guinzburg will continue the good fight, although on his own. Long live Mayer Guinzburg!
Long live Birobidjan! Long live New Birobidjan!

Then Mayer would rise, his eyes moist, his hair wind-ruffled.
He would gesticulate and move his lips, and although he
wouldn't utter a single word, we knew that he was delivering a
speech and that a crowd of little men were applauding him.
And so it went, him making speeches and us throwing up until
we finally arrived in Brazil and went to Porto Alegre, then a
small town, where we took up residence. We—Leib Kirschblum
and his family, our own family, and some others—lived in the
Caminho Novo neighborhood, in small wooden houses that had
fancifully carved eaves. At night we could hear the waters of
the Guaíba River lapping below the windows. . . . Those were
good days.

I have a photograph of those days. Here is Mayer, with his
head shaved. He had been ill with typhus and Mother had the
barber shave his head. In his photograph Mayer gazes at us with
his pale gray eyes; even though there's the trace of a smile on
his face, his hands are clenched into fists. Mayer Guinzburg, my
brother.

Father, a cabinetmaker, worked really hard. Mother looked after the house and cooked our meals. We sold fish. When there
was no fish, we sold clothes hangers, and occasionally, second-
hand clothes. Sometimes we went out pushing a small cart to
collect junk, but I'd much rather sell fish. The fish business was
good.

To me fish was just a commodity, but to Mayer Guinzburg,
fish meant much more. It was the fruit of the Comrade Fishermen's labor, of those strong, silent men, whose daily chores

Mayer had often depicted in many inspired drawings. Years later
he was to become a great fan of Dorival Caymmi, whose songs
celebrate the life and loves of the fishermen. *It's sweet to die in
the sea,* says one of those songs; *there are two loves in the life of a
fisherman,* according to another song.

It hurt Mother to see us with hamper in hand, for she had great
plans for the two of us: I would be a doctor, Mayer an engineer; or I a lawyer, Mayer an engineer; or I an engineer, Mayer
a lawyer. It soon became apparent that I had no inclinations to
books, so Mother focused her efforts on Mayer, whose problem
was of a different nature. Mayer was skinny, and it was a well-
known fact that skinny boys had a hard time getting ahead in
their studies.

And Mayer was *very* skinny. His face bones showed through
the tightly stretched skin of his face; his hard, white skull was
revealed under his clean-shaven scalp. Anybody with such a poorly
lined head would have a hard time thinking clearly. In her
search of nourishing food for Mayer, Mother displayed *diligence,
shrewdness, boldness, fearlessness, know-how, improvisation, affection.*
She pursued tender young chickens, hers and the neighbors', which
she would take in person to the *schoichet.* She was always pres-
ent at this ritual killing, thereby ascertaining herself that the di-
vine blessings had been bestowed upon the meat (especially the
breast meat, which Mayer found less loathsome). She would travel
for miles to get goat's milk—the only preventive against tuberculosis, a constant threat to skinny boys—from a certain woman,
a witch who lived in Beco do Salso. Later, when we moved to
Rua Felipe Camarão, she would go to the grocery store very early
in the morning to buy apples for Mayer. However, no matter
how early she got there, her neighbors were already ahead of her,
picking the best fruit. In order to fight her way through the
women to get to the bigger and riper apples first, Mother developed special skills: Her elbows, sinking into the bellies of the
other women, were like paddles propelling her; her voice re-

11

sounded like a siren in the fog; and her chest, as if it were the hard keel of a boat, would break open the sea of shoppers. Finally, she would reach the crate of apples. In possession of the fruit, she would run home—there to find Mayer looking disgustedly at his food. Mayer refused to eat the tasty rice that she cooked; he refused the piping hot *kneidlech,* the flavorful soup, the cookies. He would even hide himself in the attic to avoid eating. One day, quite desperate, Mother threw herself at his feet: "Tell me, son, do tell me, what would you like to eat? Mummy will give you anything you say! Even if it means taking a trip all the way to São Paulo, Mummy will get it for you."

There was a moment of silence, interrupted only by Mother's sobs.

"Pork," Mayer said finally, his eyes fixed on his plate.

"What?" Mother raised her head.

"I'd like to eat pork chops. Everybody says they're delicious."

"Everybody . . . ?"

"Everybody."

"Pork?"

"Pork."

At this point I should say a few things about Father, whose dream had been to become a rabbi. He never did, of course, but he was fervently religious. He went to the synagogue every day, kept the Sabbath, fasted several times a year. It was from this man's wife that Mayer was demanding pork.

Mother rose from her knees and left the house without a word. That evening she brought a steaming platter from the kitchen.

"What is it?" Father asked, intrigued.

"Pork chops," Mother replied.

Father dropped his fork and turned pale. Slowly he rose from the table.

"Sit down!" Mother shouted. "Can't you understand that it's the only thing he wants to eat? This skinny, weak, wretched boy. If this is what he wants to eat, then this is what he'll eat!"

"Pork!" shouted Father. "Pork in my own house! Pork in Schil Guinzburg's house!"

"Sit down!" Mother shouted again.

But Father had already left for his room, from where came the sounds of furniture being smashed amid his howls of rage. Then the front door banged shut. There was silence.

Mother emptied the platter of pork chops onto Mayer's plate.

"Eat," she said simply.

"I don't want to," Mayer muttered. "All this commotion has made me lose my appetite."

"Eat," Mother repeated.

"I don't want to. Maybe tomorrow . . ."

"Eat."

"But I don't want to, can't you understand?"

"Eat!" Mother was now shouting. "Eat! Eat!"

She began to tear her hair and to claw at her face. Quickly, Mayer began to gobble down the pork chops, and I helped him the best I could to finish them off.

From then on Mother no longer fought her way through the shoppers to get to the best apples first. She would serve him cold rice.

"Eat."

Boiled potatoes.

"Eat."

Stale bread and cookies.

"Eat."

And Mayer did eat, but every once in a while, as the family sat at the dinner table, he would needle us about the pork chops: "Ah, do I ever miss them . . ." What a rebel he was.

1919

AFTER THE RUSSIAN REVOLUTION, MAYER GUINZ-burg became even more rebellious, Avram went on. He would wake up in the middle of the night, shouting: "To the barricades!" He wouldn't call me Avram, but Comrade Brother, and he would say: "What is mine is yours, what is yours is mine—there's no private ownership anymore." He decided that we would share the same toothbrush; as a matter of fact, he discarded his. I didn't want to displease him, but I stopped brushing my teeth and for this reason I had many cavities. All of this caused Father a great deal of suffering. Father wanted Mayer to become a rabbi, so every night he placed the holy books before his son, who would open them reluctantly. Father would encourage him with words of wisdom: "Study, son, go on, study. Remember what Rabbi Yochanan ben Zacai used to say: 'You were brought up to study the Torah.'"

Mayer, drugged with sleep, would reply: "But Simeon, Rabbi Gamaliel's son, used to say: 'I've spent my life among the wise men and have learned that there is nothing better than silence. Doing, not studying, is what really counts.'"

Mayer was merely trying to provoke Father, who failing to perceive Mayer's intentions, was delighted with their polemical exchange.

"Simeon? He was inexperienced. Rabbi Gamaliel, his father, knew what he was saying when he advised his son to 'find a teacher.' I am your teacher, son."

"It is written in the Gemara," contradicted the wicked Mayer, "that 'if the disciple sees that his teacher is wrong, he should correct him.'"

Father's forehead became creased with a deep line: "What am I doing wrong, son?"

"You're forcing me to study all this nonsense when here I am fighting off sleep," Mayer shouted. "That's absurd!"

"It is also written in the Gemara," Father replied quietly, "that 'if some great man says something that sounds absurd to you, don't laugh: Try to understand him.' I'm sleepy too, but I'm staying up with you because Rabbi Hananiah ben Teradion used to say, 'Whenever two men get together to discuss the Torah, the Holy Spirit hovers over them.' We're sleepy and we're hungry, I know. But what does it matter? For it is written: 'This is how the scholar lives; he eats a chunk of bread with salt, drinks water moderately, sleeps on the floor, endures hardships.' Scholarship and religion are the greatest possible wealth we can have."

"No!" Mayer shouted. "The greatest possible wealth is to take over the sources of production, do you hear? Scholarship, religion, indeed! It's just as Marx said: Religion is the opium of the people."

"Who is this Marx?" Father would ask, perplexed. "What does he know about man's happiness?"

"Everything! He knows that hunger and injustice must be eliminated. 'Mine' and 'yours' will disappear. The new order calls for 'what is mine is yours; what is yours is mine.'"

Father would shake his head sadly.

"According to the Mishnah, there are four kinds of men: The

15

ordinary man, who says: 'What is mine is mine; what is yours is yours.' The *wicked* man, who says: 'What is mine is mine; what is yours is also mine.' I myself prefer the words of the *holy* man, who says: 'What is mine is yours; what is yours is yours.' But you, my son, say: 'What is mine is yours; what is yours is mine.' And these are the words, says the Mishnah, of the *eccentric*, a stranger among his fellow men. I'm afraid there's a lot of suffering in store for you, son."

Father was right. He did the best he could to save Mayer Guinzburg, Captain Birobidjan. That he failed wasn't his fault.

I was older and more sensible than Mayer. I was a good son. I married early and gave our parents a great number of grandchildren, all of them intelligent. (Mayer, however, always despised his nephews and nieces.) Mayer Guinzburg. "What is mine is yours; what is yours is mine." An eccentric.

1929

"CAPITALISM IS IN ITS DEATH THROES," SHOUTED Mayer Guinzburg when he heard the news about the financial crash of the New York stock market. José Goldman agreed with him enthusiastically, but Léia remained silent. She felt doubtful about it.

That year Mayer Guinzburg had been reading Rosa Luxemburg (1871–1919), whom he referred to affectionately as "my rose of Luxemburg," even though she wasn't from Luxemburg, but from Poland. While still very young she had emigrated to Germany, where she married a workman. She edited the *Arbeiterzeitung* for a while before joining the *Leipziger Volkszeitung*. She took part in the Russian Revolution of 1905. Upon her return to Germany she founded, together with Karl Liebknecht, the Spartacus party. There were arrested in January, 1919, and taken to the Moabite Prison in Berlin, where the guards killed them, allegedly while trying to escape. Their bodies, thrown into a canal, were found several days later. Rosa Luxemburg. Mayer Guinzburg wept as he read her *Letters from Prison*. Rosa

Luxemburg. Mayer Guinzburg kept a photograph of her: Her pure, lit-up face resembled Léia's. Rosa Luxemburg.

José Goldman believed that they shouldn't waste any more time establishing the collective farm. Mayer Guinzburg, however, was hesitant: He thought he would first organize a group modeled on the Spartacus League. For this purpose he recruited two friends, Berta Kornfeld and Marc Friedmann.

Marc Friedmann was a Frenchman. His father, an engineer who worked for the railroad company, had been living in Brazil for many years; he was a refined, sophisticated man. His son Marc, who wore a silk scarf around his neck, was interested in music. Berta Kornfeld was *ugly, gloomy,* and *fierce-looking;* Marc Friedmann was *cultured* and *courteous.* Although opposites, both were keen advocates of social progress.

When the group was formed, they had to face the problem of finding a suitable place to hold their meetings—a place that might later become the headquarters of their future organization. Marc Friedmann suggested the property his father owned in Beco do Salso.

"We hardly ever go there," he informed the group. "There's a big house there, unoccupied. A good place to hold our meetings, and maybe we could start our collective farm there."

In 1929 Porto Alegre was a small town. To reach Beco do Salso was quite an expedition—one had to take a narrow road winding through hills covered with wild growth; and according to Leib Kirschblum, who sometimes went as far as that area to sell goods on the installment plan, Beco do Salso wasn't exactly free of dangers. This piece of information excited Mayer Guinzburg and his comrades even more, but Léia didn't like their plan very much. However, when Berta Kornfeld made a motion that anyone refusing to go to Beco do Salso be summarily expelled from the group, Léia had no alternative but go along with them. Berta Kornfeld was ugly, gloomy and fierce-looking; she never married. She had a consuming passion for Vladimir Ilyich

Ulyanov—Lenin (1870–1924)—whose name she murmured in her sleep. Her mother, old Pessl, although insane, was frightened by this passion: "A goy, I'm sure. I bet he's married and has a drinking problem." Berta Kornfeld died of tuberculosis at a fairly young age; in her final delirium she cried out for Lenin, asking him to lie down beside her, to embrace her. The people who came to comfort her as she lay on her deathbed averted their eyes from this embarrassing scene.

1929. They'll leave someday at the break of dawn. The streets of Bom Fim will be deserted; even the old people who go to the synagogue very early in the morning won't be out yet to watch them. Stepping out of the fog, they'll assemble at the corner of Rua Henrique Dias and Rua Felipe Camarão.

One of Mayer Guinzburg's drawings depicts the beginning of this historical journey—the five comrades marching side by side, heading for Avenida Oswaldo Aranha. They are wearing short leather jackets, with gray scarves around their necks and caps on their heads. In the rucksacks on their backs, they have packed tents, blankets, clothes, books: Walt Whitman, Rosa Luxemburg.

They'll board a streetcar, get off at the end of the line, and then walk the final stretch. The houses will thin out, and then the woods—nature—will appear. They'll breathe in the pure air and smile. They'll have reached their destination.

They'll walk through the old wrought-iron gate and take the ill-kept path with shrubs growing on either side. They'll come to a large barren plain, and there, atop a small elevation, they'll see the house.

In 1929 the house will already be old.

A drawing by Mayer Guinzburg depicts it as a very big house with a wide door and many windows. Its style is vaguely colonial. It's made of good-quality materials, but the walls are peeling. Surrounded by groves and water springs.

They stand in a circle in front of the house for a brief ceremony. Still carrying the rucksacks on their backs, they listen to

Mayer Guinzburg discourse on New Birobidjan; the crops, the factories, the Palace of Culture. He ends his speech in a firm, calm voice: "At this moment we begin the building of a new society."

They shove a tall bamboo pole into the ground to be used as a flagpole, and on it they raise Léia's colorful kerchief, seeing that New Birobidjan doesn't have a flag of its own yet.

Marc Friedmann opens the door with difficulty. The house is empty except for an old brown leather couch. The floorboards are strewn with dead insects.

Mayer Guinzburg immediately divides the group into several committees: the Cleaning-up Committee; the Food Committee; and the Political Studies Committee, of which he is the chairman.

How will they spend the rest of the day? "In feverish work," Marc Friedmann will write in his journal. "Cleaning up the filth of years," Léia will write in hers. At noon they take a break and eat sandwiches. At seven o'clock they hold a meeting in order to assess their activities. The Cleaning-up Committee has cleaned and tidied the house and decorated it with posters and banners supplied by the Political Studies Committee; in addition, having completed its tasks earlier than anticipated, the committee members have erected a new flagpole—the trunk of a eucalyptus tree. Mayer Guinzburg praises their accomplishment. The Food Committee has cooked a hot, reviving dinner, and when this is announced the Political Studies Committee postpones the reading of its report, seeing that it deals with complex issues, such as productivity, the control of power, and consciousness-raising.

After dinner, they sit around a campfire and begin to sing war songs, which are followed by melancholy Yiddish songs. Finally, they lower the flag, Mayer Guinzburg delivers a brief speech on the tasks awaiting them, and they go to bed.

For the next half hour there is absolute silence in the house. Then some strange activities occur: Doors open and close, figures move about in the darkness; then a murmur of voices can be heard, the sounds of giggling and muffled outcries . . .

In the morning, as Mayer Guinzburg leaves Léia's room, he runs into Marc Friedmann.

"Did you sleep well, Marc?" Mayer asks, embarrassed. "You know, I—"

"I demand that an urgent meeting be called," Marc cuts him short, without looking at him. "With criticism and self-criticism on the agenda."

When everybody is assembled, Mayer yields the floor to Marc Friedmann, who, barely able to contain his indignation, brings up the goings-on of the previous night. "I don't want to mention any names," he begins, not looking at anyone, "but some strange things went on last night—reactionary, bourgeois things. We have come here to work, to build a new society, but instead we see that energy is being wasted on other things. That's why I make now a motion that from now on men and women sleep in separate quarters."

Mayer Guinzburg listens, at first puzzled, then suspicious, finally enraged. He waits until Marc Friedmann finishes speaking and then asks for the floor.

"First of all," he says, "Comrade Marc's accusations aren't based on facts, but merely on sounds—a murmur of voices, giggling, stealthy footsteps. Second, I have never heard it said that true love—progressive love—is wrong. Even Comrade Rosa Luxemburg loved, and she loved intensely . . ." He presents one argument after the other.

Marc Friedmann has turned pale, and by the time Mayer Guinzburg finishes his speech by challenging him to get into his self-criticism, Marc's distress reaches a climax. There are tears in his eyes as he gets to his feet. "It's not fair," he says. "It's not fair that all of you—no, I can't. José Goldman knows that I can't—that I dislike girls. I can't, I can't! What do you expect

21

me to do? Go ahead, criticize me. Yell at me, hit me, whip me until I bleed—I still can't, I can't!"

Silence follows this outburst. Then Mayer adjourns the meeting and the comrades leave.

In the afternoon they pack up their belongings and return to the city. Mayer goes home. Father, seated in his armchair, is waiting for him, a somber expression on his face.

"I don't want to discuss any of it," Mayer warns right away.

Father ignores the warning. "Mayer, son, why do you persist in tormenting me like this? You know that my greatest joy would be to see you a rabbi, a respected scholar. Your books are gathering dust . . ."

Mayer goes straight to his room, but since he is quite dirty, he doesn't dare lie down on the bed, afraid of Mother's recriminations. Fully clothed, he lies down on the floor and falls asleep. He wakes up several hours later, at dawn. He gets up. In the parlor, Father lies asleep on the brown leather couch. Mayer sees a folded sheet of paper pushed under the door. It's a note from Marc Friedmann:

> At the break of dawn, sow a field with wheat
> for me. When the future is here, when men
> become brothers and hold hands with each other,
> sow a field with wheat for me. When chil-
> dren, happy, are finally able to run freely in the
> fields, without the threat of hunger and wars,
> sow a field of wheat for me. I'll exist in the ripe
> ears of wheat . . .

"Recreant!" mutters Mayer, crumpling the paper. He goes to the kitchen to make coffee. At first he moves about slowly, full of grief, but gradually he regains his normal energy and enthusiasm. He sets a match to the firewood in the stove, then blows vigorously on the feeble flames that appear here and there. He fills the iron kettle with water. The skin on his arm, reacting to the droplets of cold water, breaks into goose pimples; his bladder demands its rights. He places the kettle on top of the stove, inside which the firewood has finally burst into flames. He opens the kitchen door and urinates upon the soil, watching the rooster perched on the garden wall, about to announce to Rua Felipe Camarão the break of a new day. "Good morning, Comrade Rooster!"

The water is boiling. He puts two, makes it three, spoonfuls of coffee into the filter, pours water over it, and the coffee is ready. From the cupboard he gets a piece of stale bread, which he eats with great relish, dunking it into his oversweetened coffee. "Good morning, Comrade Coffee! Good morning, Comrade Bread!" He turns around at a sound he hears: From the doorway, Father and Mother watch him, astonished. Mayer puts the empty cup into the sink then steps out into the backyard. He picks up a hoe, spits into his hands, chooses a spot, and starts breaking up the soil. He works nonstop, there is a lot to be done. He is going to plant a vegetable garden.

☆☆☆☆☆☆☆☆☆☆☆☆☆☆☆☆☆☆☆☆☆☆☆☆☆☆☆☆☆☆☆☆☆☆☆☆☆☆☆

1930

"**I**T WAS A TERRIBLE YEAR!" RECALLS AVRAM Guinzburg. "Father and Mother were having day-long arguments with Mayer. He refused to study, saying that getting an education was merely a device for people to gain access to a higher rank in society; and he didn't want to work either, because he was not going to help any capitalist pig get even richer."

Mother used to say that Mayer had always had a rebellious nature. When he was a young boy he refused to eat. Mother would sit in front of him, holding a bowl of soup.

"Eat."

He didn't.

Mother would pick up the spoon. Mayer would clench his teeth, shut his eyes, and sit frozen.

"Eat."

Mother would force the tip of the spoon into his mouth. Mayer could taste the soup—that good, flavorful, hot soup that Mother used to make—and yet he wouldn't open his mouth. Mother would persist with the spoon, trying to find an opening. When

24

Mayer lost a few of his milk teeth, there was a gap through which
Mother would pour some soup. After they were replaced by
permanent teeth, Mother discovered that there was a reservoir in
the area between his cheeks and his gums, a reservoir which
she found quite providential, for she believed that if she succeeded in leaving a small amount of soup there, sooner or later
Mayer would have to swallow it. However, my brother's resistance to her endeavors was incredible: I believe that he was
able to hold the soup there for minutes, hours—even days.

"Eat. Eat."

When Mother's patience showed signs of wearing thin, Father
would try to help her, but to no avail. Mayer persisted in not
opening his mouth.

"Eat!"

Mother, giving up the soup, would tempt him with bread, potatoes, steaks, noodles, meatballs, turnovers; she tried everything—
fresh, canned; hot, cold; liquids, solids. Nothing worked. Mayer
went on refusing to eat.

Sometimes he wouldn't come to the table. He had a hiding
place at the far end of the backyard, a hutlike place that he
had built with tree branches, boards and sheets of zinc. There he
would remain hidden for hours.

"Why in the world do you bury yourself there?" I would ask.

"It feels good," was his reply. "It's dark, it's cozy."

He would store a great many books there, and, as I discovered later, food as well—chunks of stale bread, slivers of old
cheese, all of which he ate with a great appetite. This kept him
alive. My guess is that the hut was the governmental palace of
some imaginary country, because at the entrance there was a pole
on which he would raise a flag. In those days Father raised a
couple of animals in the backyard. There were, if I remember
correctly, a goat—which my parents had bought from that woman
in Beco do Salso for a large sum of money—and one hen. Mayer
would talk to these creatures, to these beasts, and he even ad-

dressed the goat as "comrade." I remember one night when I woke up with a thunderstorm. Seeing that Mayer's bed was empty and that the back door was open, I went out in the rain, lamp in hand, and found Mayer and the goat in that damn hut of his. I had a hard time persuading him to come back to the house, and only succeeded after I agreed to his bringing the goat inside too.

In 1930 Mother and Father would recall such incidents during their dispirited conversations by the stove, as they ate sunflower seeds and sipped tea with plenty of sugar in it. They didn't know what to do about Mayer. Father used to buttonhole people on Rua Felipe Camarão, asking them to have a word with Mayer and explain to his son the need to work, get married, raise a good Yiddish family. People sympathized with him, but nobody dared approach Mayer, who had quite a short temper.

One day Father came home in high spirits, announcing that a famous Jewish physician, a Dr. Freud, would be arriving in Porto Alegre.

"This man," Father shouted excitedly, "has developed an amazingly successful method of effecting a cure. And without prescribing any drugs. All he uses is a leather couch and the power of words! But Dr. Freud," Father added, "will only be making a brief stopover in Porto Alegre—he's on his way to Buenos Aires—so he'll have to see Mayer right there at the airport. But it's all right because I've already ascertained that there are couches there."

"What if Mayer refuses to go?" Mother asked.

Mayer did refuse to go, saying that he didn't believe in that kind of nonsense. "But it's like the Torah, son!" Father said, anguished. "It's the power of words!"

But Mayer remained unconvinced, and so Father decided he would go alone to the airport, expound Mayer's case to Dr. Freud, and ask him for at least some advice.

Dr. Freud arrived in Porto Alegre on Christmas Eve, the

time of the year when Father, working overtime, earned some extra money, but even so, he believed he should drop everything and go to the airport.

He got there even before the arrival of the welcome committee, made up of illustrious citizens: Community leaders, doctors, professors. Carrying a picture of Dr. Freud that he had cut out of a magazine, Father scurried about, annoying people with his nervousness.

Finally, the airplane landed and Dr. Freud entered the airport lobby. Pushing and shoving, Father succeeded in getting near the famous man.

"My name is Guinzburg, Dr. Freud," Father said, grabbing the hand of the founder of psychoanalysis. "I came here especially to talk to you. It wasn't easy, you know, sir, today being Christmas Eve ..."

Dr. Freud was flabbergasted. "I'm sorry, my good man, but—"

Father cut him short. "I know what you're about to say: That you're just passing through on your way to Buenos Aires. I know, I'm a well-informed man. I'm familiar with your career, I hold a high opinion of you, I think you'll get to the top of the ladder ... but you have to listen to me."

Dr. Freud was glancing around him, as if asking for help, when Dr. Finkelstein, a physician in Bom Fim who knew Father, decided to intervene. He took Father by the arm, to lead him away. "Let's go, Mr. Guinzburg. Come and talk to me ..."

"Please!" Father shouted, extricating himself. "I'd like to have a word with Dr. Freud, if you don't mind, or is it only you people who have this right? I'm a person too. I'm a Jew with a problem! Isn't that so, Dr. Freud?"

"But the airplane ..." said Dr. Freud, embarrassed.

"The airplane can wait. Airplanes can't tell us what to do. Problems come first. Dr. Freud, you'll have to listen to me. You can't imagine, sir, how I've been looking forward to this moment. When I learned about your arrival, I said to my wife,

27

'I'm sure Dr. Freud will be able to solve our problem. Mayer doesn't want to go—that's right, no, that's wrong, he should go, but I'll explain the case to Dr. Freud and he'll come up with a solution. He'll use the power of words and, if necessary, one of the couches in the airport.' Dr. Freud, I'm willing to lie down on a couch if you want me to. I know all about your great abilities, Dr. Freud. You remind me a lot of a rabbi we had in Russia, a really wonderful rabbi. We would tell him our problems, he would close his eyes, think for a moment, and behold! he would tell people what they had to do. He was never wrong! Marital problems, problems between parents and children, problems with money and poor health—you name it, and he'd always find a solution. And he wasn't even a writer! That's what I've said to my wife, 'Dr. Freud is not only a speaker but a writer as well—*The Ego and the Id, Totem and Tabu*' ... As you can see, sir, I'm familiar with your work."

Sigmund Freud was born in Freiburg, Moravia, in 1856 and had lived in Vienna since he was four years old. He had studied with Charcot and worked with Breuer. He discovered the unconscious. He evolved the free association method. He wrote *The Psychopathology of Everyday Life, The Interpretation of Dreams,* and *Wit and Its Relation to the Unconscious.* In 1930 he made a stopover in Porto Alegre, and while at the airport, he was accosted by Father, from whom he now wanted to escape, asking the bystanders to intervene. Despite their best efforts to lead Father away, they didn't succeed.

"Dr. Freud," Father was saying without letting go of the visitor's sleeve, "it's like this: I have this son ... I'll explain everything in a moment, Dr. Freud, and I'm sure you'll understand and be able to tell me what to do. My son, well, he—I'd like him to become a rabbi. As you might know, sir, there are no rabbis in Porto Alegre, and being a rabbi is an honorable occupation, don't you think so, Dr. Freud? Something similar to what you do, listening and offering advice, except that a rabbi doesn't use a couch but deep down it all amounts to the same thing, doesn't it? So I want him to—but he ... he has a rebellious nature. He doesn't want to do anything—doesn't want to study, doesn't want to work, he's been like this ever since he was a young child. His mother would say 'Eat! Eat!' but he wouldn't, not even the soup, the good soup that his mother made. Isn't he mean, Dr. Freud? Yes, he is, and a rebel to boot, I assure you, and I ..."

Passengers were being asked over the public address system to board the plane. Dr. Freud picked up his suitcase and began to take leave of the bystanders. Father, following him on his heels, kept talking nonstop.

"... And last year, Dr. Freud, he hid himself in the woods, together with some friends of his—one is that José Goldman, a shameless left-winger—and they even took girls out there with them. Disgraceful, don't you think, sir? And good Jewish girls they were too, from good families. Isn't it outrageous? Ah, Dr. Freud, if you want me to, I'll tell you some of his dreams, because he talks in his sleep. He's probably gotten a guilty conscience about upsetting his parents the way he does, when we have nothing but his welfare in mind. He talks in his sleep and I go to his bedroom and write down everything he says. I didn't even know why I was doing this but now I do, it was a premonition I had that you'd come to Porto Alegre someday and that I'd consult you about this son of mine and if you needed one of his dreams for interpretation, I'd be able to supply you with one or several dreams, all written down ..."

Dr. Freud was trying to get to the departure gate but Father wouldn't let him.

"... I can't pay you, Dr. Freud, for this consultation," Father went on. "That is, I can't pay you much, but I know you won't charge me your usual fee—I know you charge a fortune, you wouldn't be able to do all this flying if you didn't make a lot of money—after all, this consultation was quick, held here at the

29

airport and I didn't even lie down on the couch, and besides, you're a Jew like me and you're going to give me a discount, aren't you? I don't make much money, just enough to make ends meet, enough to feed and clothe my wife and sons, even that Mayer, this rebel, who's telling you a lie if he says I don't give him any food, that's a lie, because I do, and his mother was always insisting that he eat, eat, and if he didn't, it was because he didn't want to—"

Dr. Freud, visibly furious now, stopped walking. He turned to Father and shouted: "But don't you see that I can't possibly listen to you now?" His words startled Father, who went as far as to take one step back.

"But, Dr. Freud—"

"Why don't you consult a psychiatrist here in Porto Alegre?"

"No, Dr. Freud," said Father, in a dejected tone of voice. "I couldn't do that. Not when I know that you're the best, and you don't really think that I'd settle for anything but the very best where my son, my very own son, is concerned, do you? No, Dr. Freud, no. Bear with me, sir, and please don't ask me to see some other doctor, for you'll as good as insult me if you do. I'm poor, yes, but I have my pride."

Father was overcome by emotion. He was trembling. He took a handkerchief out of his pocket and wiped his tears.

And Dr. Freud pitied him. "Listen, I intend to return to Porto Alegre someday, and maybe next time . . ."

Father laughed sadly.

"You're trying to deceive me, Dr. Freud, I know you are . . . but I'm not all that stupid, sir. I know you won't be back. You're a busy man, sir, you have your commitments, your patients. I work too, I know how it is. No, sir, you won't be back. Besides . . ."

Father put his mouth to Dr. Freud's ear.

"I've heard that you have cancer and won't live much longer."

Dr. Freud turned pale. Father took one step back, putting his hand over his mouth.

"Oh God! Oh no, what have I said? Maybe you didn't even know about it. Please, do forgive me, Dr. Freud. Actually, I lied. Yes, I told you a lie, Dr. Freud. It was a joke, I often speak in jest. Well, no, it wasn't a joke really, I mean, it was a deliberate trick, I was trying to trick you into listening to me ..."

Dr. Freud was being repeatedly called over the public address system. Father picked up the doctor's suitcase and followed him.

"Are you going to board the plane as well?" asked Dr. Freud, taken aback.

"No, but I'm walking you to the plane so that I can finish telling you about my son."

Dr. Freud was waving at his friends and Father kept on talking.

"Whenever I discussed the Torah with my son, he would talk back to me, twisting the meaning of the holy words ..."

They were walking on the tarmac.

"He derides the Gemara, the Mishnah. What do you think of a son who behaves so badly to his father?"

They reached the gangway. The stewardess asked Dr. Freud for his boarding pass and he was groping in his pockets for it.

"And you, sir?" she asked Father.

"A friend of Dr. Freud's, just escorting him to the plane," Father explained, and then lowering his voice he turned to Dr. Freud: "I don't want her to know that I am here to consult you. I'd hate for people to discuss my family's problems. You understand, don't you, Dr. Freud?"

"I understand," said Dr. Freud. "My suitcase, please."

"Well, Dr. Freud, now that you know all there's to know about my son, I'd like your advice. You know, this neighbor of mine—a tailor, and a very intelligent man, but very cynical too—read a book about you and he claims that he knows what's wrong with my son. It's a complex, he says. Do tell me, Dr. Freud, does my son have a complex?"

"Maybe he does," shouted Dr. Freud from the top of the stairs and then he boarded the plane.

"Maybe? Then it's possible that he *doesn't* have a complex. I've always said that this tailor didn't know what he was talking about!"

The plane took off. Father stood waving at Dr. Freud, who disappeared into the clouds.

Whenever recounting this conversation to his friends, Father would praise Dr. Freud lavishly.

"A great doctor," he would say, "a great scholar. He put his finger right on my son's problem. And I'll tell you something else: His fees are quite reasonable."

1933

FINALLY, MAYER GUINZBURG HAD NO CHOICE BUT
to find a job. He got a job working for Leib Kirschblum's father, who was quite an old man then. He owned a small no-
tions store in Bom Fim, called The Favorite, which sold silk
embroidery thread, silk braid, elastic, yarn, remnants of percale, lingerie.

The store was like a dark cellar, cool in the summer but icy
in the winter. People entered through a low door and picked
their way around the hampers of remnants to the counter at the
back of the store. There stood Mayer Guinzburg, his spiritless
eyes fixed on the street. Leib Kirschblum's father stood at the
cash register, nodding off, but the slightest noise would jerk
him awake: "Yes, sir, can I help you ...? Mayer! Mayer!" "There's
nobody here, Mr. Kirschblum," Mayer would mutter in an acid
tone of voice. Then in the winter of 1933, when the old man
became ill, and Dr. Finkelstein ordered him to stay home, Mayer
Guinzburg was saddled with running the store, a task that wasn't
too difficult, however, since the customers were few and far
between.

He would open the store very early in the morning. Sometimes the fog coming from Redenção invaded the store, and in the surrounding dimness Mayer felt as if he were afloat in the sea, half-drowned. Once in a while he would put the boxes of buttons in order and tidy the shelves. Gradually lassitude would come over him and he would see a crowd of little men standing on the counter. They smiled at him. At first Mayer abhorred the little creatures and tried to chase them away by brandishing the yellow wooden yardstick at them. Little by little, however, he got used to their presence, especially after noticing that not only did they listen to his grumbling but also seemed to support him. "That filthy old bastard; that capitalist exploiter." The little men nodded their approval. "If he could, he would suck the blood out of the workers!" The little men applauded. "We must fight back!" Another round of applause. If a customer entered the store, the little men disappeared. Grudgingly, Mayer would sell the shopper a length of elastic.

Gradually he became acquainted with the other inhabitants of the store. Behind of a bolt of cretonne lived a spider, who had a small body and long, delicate legs; she moved brazenly about the shelves. There was also a mouse, who would sometimes pop his head out of a small hole in the baseboard. And finally, inside an empty box, Mayer met an insect whose name he didn't know: He was bigger than an ant and smaller than a cockroach, and of an indefinite color. Those were his comrades, and they kept him company through the long, empty afternoons.

If old Kirschblum were to die, Mayer is thinking, I would shut down the store and start an entirely new life right here. He'll put the small backyard—now a filthy place, a dumping ground for cardboard boxes, pieces of wood and rusty cans—to good use. Mayer Guinzburg will clear it of all that garbage, and the earth, once cleared, will receive tender loving care. He will break up the soil so as to bury the old crust and uncover the fresh earth; then he will sow. The earth will show its gratitude: soon the exuberant buds, bursting with energy, will be sprouting all over. There will be plants everywhere; everywhere, except by the flag-pole, on which every morning Mayer Guinzburg will raise the flag of New Birobidjan. As for the store, it will be cleaned out: the entire stock of silk embroidery thread, silk braid, elastic, yarn, remnants of percale, lingerie will be hurled into a paved lot, where they'll lie in a gigantic heap and then be made into a bon-fire; and in the black smoke rising to the sky, Mayer Guinzburg will see his liberation.

"Never again in a speck of society!" he'll shout. "Onward, pro-ductive forces!"

The store will be partitioned off; the Palace of Culture will be located in one section; the headquarters of the Political Com-mittee in another section; the editorial room of *The Voice of New Birobidjan* in the remaining section. In this great enterprise Mayer Guinzburg will be backed up by Comrade Spider, Comrade Mouse, and Comrade Insect. Mayer Guinzburg will be fond of Comrade Spider and Comrade Mouse, but he'll dislike Comrade Insect; he won't be able to explain why, but he'll dislike him. He'll try very hard to like him, but he won't succeed. Even self-criticism won't do any good. Maybe because Comrade Insect will always remain indefinite, neither ant nor cockroach; and this kind of ambiguity, as Mayer Guinzburg knows well, will even-tually translate itself into ideological deviations. Standing on the speakers' platform, under the portrait of Rosa Luxemburg, Mayer Guinzburg will say in a speech: "Comrade Insect persists in mak-ing the same serious mistakes!"

He is roused from these dreams by a few customers, who are rare but demanding. Annoyed, he waits on them. When will the moment of decision arrive? he wonders.

Suddenly. It arrived suddenly one winter afternoon. As he sat behind the counter, half-submerged in boredom, he felt his de-cision like a jolt. He got up, went to the door, and closed it. Then he turned to the shelves and said in a firm voice:

"At this moment we begin the building of a new society."

The little men broke into applause. Mayer took off his jacket, rolled up his shirt sleeves. He was about to clean up the place when there was a knock at the door. At first he pretended he hadn't heard, but the knocking, now frantic, wouldn't stop, so he went and opened the door.

It was Léia, in tears.

"My father has died, Mayer."

Half a year later, they were married.

1934

OLD KIRSCHBLUM WAS VERY DECENT: AS A WEDding gift, he offered Mayer partnership in the store. Pressed by the responsibilities of marriage, Mayer accepted, even though he had no desire to spend his life behind a counter. Léia, however, was full of plans for the store. To begin with, she gave the place a good cleaning, during which Comrade Insect and Comrade Spider were slain with repeated blows of the broom. Comrade Mouse met with an even sadder fate: Léia was putting the shelves in order when Comrade Mouse decided to stick his head outside the hole. Léia let out a scream and fled. Later, when Mayer came upon Comrade Mouse's dead body, he saw that the little creature's heart had given out; after all, Mayer thought sadly, he was getting on in years and the emotional stress had been more than he could take. Mayer buried him under the heap of old boxes, pieces of wood and rusty cans at the far end of the small yard.

The new stock, the carefully arranged displays in the show windows, and the front door now open at all times, soon attracted customers. Mayer would stand behind the cash register, looking alert: "Yes, sir! Léia! Léia!"

Before long he was able to buy out old Kirschblum. Business was good and Mayer didn't fear the competition. He waited on the customers, a bitter smile on his lips.

There was, however, one obstacle blocking the road to wealth: the threatening appearances of an inspector from the Revenue Department. This evil-looking man would show up when least expected, demanding to see the account books and the sales slips. He fined Mayer ruthlessly on several occasions, but Mayer soon devised ways of cheating the inspector. This he would do with an impassive face, reassuring himself: A representative from the oppressing classes, which must be defeated. And when they are finally defeated, we'll begin the building of a new society.

Léia had grown big and solid. She assisted Mayer in running the store and also looked after their home—always doing her work with energy, as she put it. She would nudge her husband whenever, in the midst of doing something, he stopped to stare at a spot over the balcony, moving his lips and making gestures, which although restrained, were quite vehement.

Time flowed. Like a river, time flowed. On Sunday mornings Mayer Guinzburg, like a log carried in the current, walked slowly along Rua Felipe Camarão. This river, the Felipe Camarão, flowed into the sea, the Bom Fim. In this sea Mayer Guinzburg found himself afloat, half-drowned. From the beach, Avram Guinzburg and his children, and his friends Leib Kirschblum and José Goldman greeted him. Mayer would reply, his voice sounding distant because his ears were immersed in water, while the mouth spoke from the surface. Many years went by in this way.

☆☆

1935, 1936, 1937, 1938, 1939, 1940, 1941, 1942

MAYER GUINZBURG'S NEPHEWS AND NIECES WOULD look at him, in amazement. "Uncle is weird," they would say to Avram. They made fun of him, calling him "Captain Biro-bidjan."

Mayer pretended he didn't hear. Many years later the nephews and nieces heard that someone was planning to write a book about their uncle.

"Uncle was a crackpot," one of them, the psychiatrist, said. "A schizoid? A manic-depressive? I don't know, I really don't know. Quite frankly, I wouldn't be able to tell you. It was such a long time ago ... I don't know, frankly, I don't. I would have to ... anyhow, it's too late now. It was a long time ago ... I don't know."

"They're thinking of bringing this book out as a series of modules," said another nephew, the architect. "Interesting. Each module would correspond to a particular year, I suppose, or to a cluster of years, or maybe to a phase in Uncle's life."

"Uncle was an unforgettable character," said a niece, the social worker. "There was a certain poetry in his gestures ... When somebody writes down the history of Bom Fim, they should include a chapter on Mayer Guinzburg. I remember his great affection for animals. There's a phrase of his that became imprinted on my mind: 'Sula, the goat, is a useful animal.' Many people find goats loathsome, but Uncle never felt they were."

"A book?" said another nephew, the adman, knitting his brows. "But will it sell? There's more than the commercial aspect to be considered. Of course, I'm interested in this aspect too, but after all, there's more to it than a few extra cruzeiros ... what I mean is, it needs to be promoted. Will people read it? Well, they might. Maybe an attractive dust jacket, with an interesting blurb; something like: 'Congratulations, Dear Reader, on having purchased this book, which will give you many educational and entertaining hours. Who was Birobidjan? A hero? A wise man? A poet? Read and find out for yourself, and don't be at all surprised if you see that this fascinating character embodies all of these aspects ...' "

Mayer Guinzburg fathered a son. When the child was born, he wanted to name him Spartacus, in memory of the Spartacus party, founded by Karl Liebknecht and Rosa Luxemburg. But Léia preferred Jorge, and Mayer Guinzburg finally agreed to her choice, but in his mind he called the child Spartacus. Léia didn't think much of her husband's opinions, and when annoyed with him, she would call him Captain Birobidjan, and so did everyone else in Bom Fim. However, both of them were of one mind about the boy's education. Léia would read books aloud to him. Passages from Antônio Barata's *The Pirates' Book:* "... motionless, half-drowned, he lay afloat ..."

Mayer Guinzburg would have preferred Jorge Amado. He wasn't absolutely sure that pirates were progressive. True, these sea-robbers stole from the rich; however, they didn't give any of their booty to the poor. He regarded them with suspicion.

Ah, hard times were those! An abortive communist uprising; the civil war in Spain; the outbreak of World War II ...

What did those times consist of? Four seasons. Summer, always hot in Porto Alegre, when Léia would sigh for the beaches of Capão da Canoa; autumn, when they thought of buying a new house; winter, when the fog rolled in from Redenção; spring ... Four seasons.

Mayer Guinzburg hadn't been feeling well. Something vague, something like a weight on his chest. He went to Dr. Finkelstein. "There's a new treatment for this nowadays ..." said Dr. Finkelstein. "The patient is asked to lie down on a couch and then he talks on and on ..." He prescribed some tablets. They were white and small and tasted somewhat bitter. Mayer would take one out of the bottle and examine it carefully.

"My life," he would say to Léia, "is like this tablet—flattened out, white, bitter ..."

"Swallow it," Léia would reply, "and then eat. The soup's very good."

Léia ate well. She couldn't afford to be undernourished, for she worked hard and had to keep up her strength. She wasn't given to complaining, but there were times when she could taste bitterness in her mouth. "Life is bitter," she would murmur. She alleviated her sorrows with Neugebauer chocolates. But by and large she had things under control, although occasionally she was overcome by the desire to cut herself off from the world and disappear. Her eyes would close but soon open again; and over the years this movement grew increasingly faster, until it developed into a tic, a constant blinking of the eyes that became her trademark. At times she was weighed down with her great responsibilities, heavy like the burden a horse carries on its back; then she would feel a pain in her kidneys, but only as a last resort would she go to Dr. Finkelstein, who would prescribe some white pills that she invariably forgot to take. Léia. Her blond

41

hair began to turn gray even before the birth of their second child, a daughter.

Mayer wanted to name her Rosa. "Why?" asked Léia, intrigued. Mayer was about to reply, moved by the desire to recall the old days; tears began to well up and his lips parted. But he said nothing. They were at the table, and he contented himself with making drawings on the tablecloth with his knife. "We'll call her Raquel," said Léia. "Eat," she added. Mayer rose from the table without having touched his steak. Léia's right hand was shaking. This would happen at times: Whenever Mayer annoyed her and whenever Jorge cried in the night or wet his bed, her right hand felt like striking, but her head, cooler, wouldn't let it; the hand would move forward, then backward; forward, then backward. This movement soon turned into a tremor, at first crude, then gradually becoming more refined until it was perfected into the delicate vibrations seen in the wings of insects or in the legs of spindly spiders—a tic that became another trademark for her. Léia. She didn't sleep well; restless, she would toss about in bed—just as she had at the age of twelve, when expelled from night's repose by certain dreams, she would wake up in the middle of the night, drenched in sweat. Léia.

On their eighth wedding anniversary, Mayer took her out to dinner at the Restaurant Guaraxaim. Before the soup was brought to the table, they kissed; slowly, softly, they kissed. Mayer closed his eyes and saw New Birobidjan, the crops, the comrade animals, the flagpole, the Palace of Culture. He was about to talk about them, but at that moment the waiter came. Léia ordered something; then Mayer ordered something. She ordered two other things; he ordered one more. Then Léia ordered two additional things, and Mayer, in a surprising display of aggressiveness, ordered three other things. Out of the ten orders, the waiter delivered five quite efficiently and three not so efficiently. Claiming forgetfulness, this waiter failed to deliver two of their orders, namely: (1) bread, and (2) napkins. Mayer didn't insist too much on having the bread, which would make him fat, according to Dr. Finkelstein. Mayer wasn't as thin as he used to be. In his belt, the number of holes to the right of the buckle kept increasing, whereas the number of holes to the left of the buckle kept decreasing. Mayer suspected that the proportion of, say, five to three holes marked the boundary line, beyond which lay the territory inhabited by the corpulent bourgeoisie. He thought he would avoid this evidence by wearing suspenders, even though they were a symbol of retrogression. Léia would criticize him for worrying about such things. "Eat," she would say; she wanted to see him strong, not elegant. Leanness worried her. She was aware, of course, that fat people didn't live as long as thin people; but this was a problem to worry about later, at the time when death arrived. At mealtime she wanted Mayer to eat soup, bread, enough of everything. She complained to the waiter; Mayer didn't. She kicked up a fuss over the napkins; her hands were dirty and she couldn't wipe them clean.

"What do you think I am, a pig?" she shouted.

The waiter stood listening, his head bowed. Mayer noticed that his eyes were riveted on a spot over the table and that his lips were moving. Mayer thought he heard the waiter say: "Yes, Comrade Pig. I think so too, Comrade Pig."

But how did he dare mock him? A mere waiter, an employee, a servant—a slave so to speak—using the name of an impure animal to insult him! This was disrespect, defiance, even anti-Semitism!

"With the likes of him one must crack the whip!" remarked a fat man sitting at the next table. The man's lips were smeared with grease and he had a napkin around his neck.

That was it: only by cracking the whip. How could one begin the building of a better world—Mayer thought with a pang of anguish—with people like this waiter? He was distressed and not feeling well; whether the reason was overeating or despondency, he couldn't tell. And this was happening at a moment when it was important that he remain cool and collected. The bill was already on the table and he had to verify the accuracy of the numerous items and, what was even worse, figure out how much of a tip to leave. It was quite taxing to maintain his poise while trying to devise a way to punish the waiter without arousing in him thoughts of revenge. For Mayer intended to become a regular at the Guaraxaim and didn't want to be an object of the waiters' hatred; Mayer had heard it said that they had their revenge on the customers by spitting on their food. On the other hand, Mayer felt he had to punish the waiter for his inefficiency, which amounted to twenty, maybe even fifty percent; so he could perhaps reduce the tip by half. If Mayer were to add the waiter's impertinence to his inefficiency, the tip could be eliminated altogether; and if he took all these various factors into consideration, Mayer would be quite justified in demanding a discount. However, he wouldn't go that far; he would leave a tip, because—among several other reasons—he was a store owner, and it would please him to overhear people remark as he left the restaurant: "That Mayer is sure doing well." The waiter, after all, was a poor devil, a wretched drunk who probably had syphilis too. One of the scum of society. Mayer kept fiddling with the coins on the saucer, lifting them and putting them back again.

"What in the world are you doing?" asked Léia, impatient. "Let's go, the children must be getting restless."

Mayer got up. The waiter helped him with his overcoat.

"Good-bye, Captain."

Captain? Captain Birobidjan? Mayer Guinzburg turned around, furious. The waiter had an obsequious smile on his face.

"Don't you ever call me 'Captain' again, do you hear?"

" 'Boss,' then, all right? 'Boss' is all right, isn't it? I knew you wouldn't object to 'boss'! Good-bye, boss! Best wishes! You too, missus!"

Ah, hard times were those! In Europe they were fighting the Nazis, José Goldman was burning with indignation. He had been taking boxing lessons and one day in front of Serafim's bar he got into a scuffle with a member of the right-wing Integralista party, a fellow named Colomy.

"All Jews are communists!" the Integralista kept shouting, as he slapped José Goldman in the face.

"That's a lie!" José Goldman replied, jabbing at him.

"Oh, yeah? And Marx? What about him?" said the Integralista while attempting a stranglehold.

"Marx was an assimilated Jew!" and José Goldman freed himself, giving the other man a right cross.

"And Trotsky? What about him?" Colomy was now trying to aim a kick at him.

"A renegade!" said José Goldman, dodging and giving him a right hook.

"So, Jews are good for nothing, then!" The Integralista was now running for his life. "They deny their own race."

"Scoundrel!" José Goldman wanted to chase him and give him one of his deadly uppercuts but his friends held him back.

From a distance, Colomy shouted: "Jews are communists!"

"I wish they were," muttered José Goldman. "I wish they were."

Ah, such hard times! At Léia's insistence, Mayer joined the Israelite Social Circle; and since he didn't know how to dance, he took dancing lessons from an Italian instructor, who assured Mayer he would be able to master the fox-trot, the maxixe, the rumba, the tango, and the conga in a week. The lessons took place at the instructor's home on Rua Duque de Caxias. There, in the semidarkness of the parlor, he would hold Mayer by the waist and try to press his cheek against Mayer's. It's only for one week, Mayer would say to himself, disgusted. Only for one week.

That's what those years were like.

Mayer Guinzburg spent the day working in the store; in the evening he collected the money from the cash register, went home, had dinner, and got into his pajamas. Seated on the bed, he counted the day's income, moistening his fingertips in the glass of water left by the bedside especially for this purpose. One night he dreamed that he was working in the fields under a blazing sun, supervised by the waiter from the Guaraxaim, who waved a huge whip at him. He woke up startled, and feeling thirsty, drained off the glass of water. In the morning, when he realized what he had done, he wanted to throw up, but couldn't.

Ah, such hard times! Mayer Guinzburg worked hard and there was no time left to draw. During all those years he had made one single drawing—a self-portrait in which he is depicted as a lean man with a stoop (and an incipient paunch), a shock of hair (resistant to all attempts to have it controlled with Gumex), a cigarette held in his fingers (a heavy smoker: over three packs a day). When he attempted to sketch Rosa Luxemburg's face, he realized that her features, once so familiar to him, were already fading from his mind. He put the sketchbook aside.

In 1939, the Republicans were defeated in Spain.

Of that war, Mayer Guinzburg will keep, in addition to bitter memories, the words of the song "El Ejército del Ebro," Hemingway's book *For Whom the Bell Tolls,* and a photograph by Robert Capa showing a soldier at the moment when he was hit by Falangist bullets. The expression of pain on that man's face was what Mayer could see when he looked at himself in the mirror every morning.

In 1942, Mayer Guinzburg fell ill with hepatitis. He spent a long time in bed, thinking about death, although according to Dr. Finkelstein, the disease was not serious. "My life is empty," Mayer would say to Léia when she brought him soup. "Eat," his wife would reply. From the top of the chest of drawers, the little men watched him in silence. Avram and his children would visit him, but wouldn't get too close for fear of contamination. José Goldman sent him a book by Mayakovsky, saying that Mayer didn't have to return it. Mayer suspected that like everybody else José Goldman was afraid of catching the disease. Marc Friedmann came by with a tall, dark-complexioned young man, but Léia turned them away at the door. Leib Kirschblum spread rumors about the store going out of business. "My father knew how to run a business," he would say with a smile. "Even when sick, he never missed a day's work." Having no appetite for food, and no strength even to lift a finger, Mayer stayed in bed, thinking of Birobidjan: What were the Jews doing in those fertile lands? He felt sad and depressed. It was the hepatitis.

1942. Stalingrad was resisting the Nazis.

1942. Mayer Guinzburg isn't sure yet but he knows that he'll end up by doing it: On the thirty-seventh day of his illness he'll jump out of bed, all his fatigue gone. He'll get dressed quietly, keeping an eye on Léia, who will be asleep; he'll put on his old pants and an old shirt, boots, the leather jacket. Quickly he'll pack the rucksack and won't forget to include books: Michael Gold's *Jews Without Money*, Howard Fast's *Freedom Road*, Mayakovsky's and Walt Whitman's works, his own sketchbook, José Goldman's "Song to Birobidjan." He'll go to the children's room; kissing them on the forehead, he'll murmur: "Farewell, Spartacus. Farewell, Rosa Luxemburg." He'll open the front door, will gaze for a moment at the houses on Rua Felipe Camarão, will fill his lungs with the fresh early morning air, and will set out.

1942. He reaches Avenida Oswaldo Aranha, feels hungry, and it occurs to him that he hasn't eaten properly in over a month. He enters the Serafim and orders coffee, bread, and butter. He eats hungrily, gathering strength for the long journey that lies ahead. The taxi drivers watch him in surprise.

"Joining the war, are you, Captain?"

Mayer hesitates. He wonders if it will be worthwhile to climb onto the counter and make a speech: just a few words, but full of fire, of inspiration. *"There are many wars, Comrade Taxi Drivers. In some we fight alone ..."*

He finishes off his coffee and leaves. The first workers are already out on the street, on their way to work. Mayer looks at them with envy: These are the men to whom the future belongs; they are following the right road. He, however, was born and raised in a speck of society, in a tiny hole where the sun never shone, where he spent many years of his life, half-suffocated, speaking in a low voice and then only to insects and other small animals. Now this historical error will be corrected.

1942. The Russians resist the Nazi advance. Mayer recalls General Budenny and his cossacks, whose hymn Mayer learned from a Spaniard:

> *"Galopando caminos de coraje y valor,*
> *ginetes vuelan como huracán.*
> *A las armas! resuena desde el Volga al Kubán,*
> *la ardiente voz del clarín vengador!*
>
> *Sol y polvo Budieni los dirige, allá ván*
> *En feros potros de espuma y sudor*
> *Aguardando la voz del comandante que diga*
> *Adelante, a luchar y a vencer!"*

Singing softly, Captain Birobidjan gets on a streetcar.

The conductor eyes him distrustfully: "Going camping?"

Birobidjan considers taking advantage of this opportunity to indoctrinate Comrade Conductor, but chooses instead to nod in agreement; he keeps on singing softly. The conductor watches him in the mirror.

The captain gets off at the end of the line. From there, he will proceed on foot. Birobidjan illustrated this journey in a series of drawings collected in the album "The One-Man Army." The *first drawing* depicts his arrival at Marc Friedmann's country place in Beco do Salso. From the top of the hill, Birobidjan gazes at the city lying at his feet; his face reveals *courage, determination,* and a certain *stoicism;* his clenched fists evince strength; and his boots are firmly planted on the ground. The property hadn't been looked after in years. Marc Friedmann hadn't set foot there since his father's death. The place brings back sad memories. The gate is secured with a chain and a huge pad-lock. The *second drawing* depicts Birobidjan at work on destroy-ing these ancient symbols of ownership. His hands hold a rock; his lips are parted in a jubilant smile at the sight of the pad-lock beginning to yield. From a distance, a horse looks on in amazement.

Then, making his way through the dense thicket, the captain reaches the house. It looks even more ramshackle than it did the first time he saw it. The years—1929, 1930 ... 1935 ... that dismal year 1939—have played havoc with it. The captain walks around the house; peering through the broken windowpanes, he sees filth and desolation. He decides not to go in. He has brought a small tent; he'll sleep in it. With the tools he finds in the shed, he clears the yard in front of the house. Piercing the fog, the sun begins to warm the land. The captain takes off his leather jacket, and, a moment later, his shirt. "My naked torso, cov-ered with the sweat of a new life, glistens in the sun," he says to himself. He cuts down a eucalyptus tree, lops off all branches and twigs, inserts the tree into the hole previously dug, and behold—the flagpole! The *third drawing* depicts the raising of the flag of New Birobidjan. It's a white flag on which the cap-tain painted the letter *N* and *B* intertwined with a plow, a hoe, a power lathe, a painter's palette, a telescope, a book, and a test tube.

The sun illuminates Captain Birobidjan's face. He is a man in his mid-thirties, with pale eyes and a characteristic Jewish nose. He is rather thin. He is growing a beard, which will become full, like Marx's and Freud's. The wind ruffles this pioneer's hair, while the flag slowly rises on the pole. At the end of the cere-

49

mony, the captain says in a low but very clear tone of voice: "We now begin the building of a new society."

Crowded together on a trunk overturned on the ground, the little men applaud enthusiastically.

In the *fourth drawing* night has fallen. Seated by a campfire, the captain sings nostalgic songs as he gets dinner ready. There won't be any: The milk will turn sour, the coffee will get spilled, the bread will fall on the ground and get dirty, the butter will run.

With an empty stomach, the captain crawls into the tent. Above him, the starry sky; beneath his body, the earth, ancient and mysterious. And everywhere, insects: crickets, fireflies, mosquitoes; and who knows, spiders and scorpions and maybe snakes too. The captain wraps the blanket more tightly around him. His eyes fill with tears; his stomach rumbles. "Léia! Léia!" he murmurs. "Jorge, Raquel." He misses them already, but he knows that the top of the mountain is a lonesome place. He knows that in the course of this journey it will be necessary for him to burn bridges. He cries himself to sleep.

The days that follow will witness some feverish activities in New Birobidjan. It is the planting season, and the settler begins to sow corn and beans in the black, humid soil. As he toils, his heartbeat increases and his breath comes faster; he yearns to see the first leaves. He'll treat the plants as friends. The corn plant and the bean plant will back him in this great enterprise: the corn plant, *pure, frank,* and *loyal;* the bean plant, somewhat *secretive*—but both of them good comrades. The harvest season will bring him pain: to pluck the soft ears of corn and the beautiful pods ... yes, he'll have to, but he won't sell them in the market; he won't subject these gentle vegetables to the law of supply and demand. He'll eat them and thus become part of nature's eternal cycle.

The captain won't devote himself exclusively to the raising of crops. His is a pastoral temperament. So, one day he returns

50

home—one of the rare occasions when he absents himself from New Birobidjan—with a pig, a goat, and a hen: Comrade Pig, Comrade Goat, and Comrade Hen.*

Comrade Goat. The captain would milk her, and when he was finished she would thank him and offer him the warm, frothy milk. This healthful beverage had protected many people against tuberculosis. Birobidjan would rather drink milk than any-thing else.

As for Comrade Hen ... Comrade Hen was a great disap-pointment to Birobidjan. She was high-strung, touchy, and cack-led incessantly but unproductively; she never laid any eggs. She didn't pull her weight. When her back was turned to him, Birobidjan would watch her with rancor; when she was facing him, however, he would do his best to treat her well and he would even smile at her—which was becoming increasingly more difficult to do. As the days went by, Birobidjan, who ate fru-gally, began to miss eating meat. Never once did it occur to him to take the life of the useful Comrade Goat or of the friendly Comrade Pig; however, it was with the greatest difficulty that he overcame the desire to wring Comrade Hen's neck. In some of his dreams Comrade Hen would appear as a colossal animal, capable of yielding tons of breasts and legs; he would chase her, letting out atavistic screams.† He would wake up from these dreams feeling ashamed and ready for self-criticism. "I do ad-mit, Comrade Hen, that I've allowed myself to be controlled by ideas that are retrograde and already overcome ..." He tried to convince himself that a vegetarian diet was progressive, and a

---

*George Orwell describes a similar situation in *Animal Farm;* however, his animals do not feel any empathy with human beings. They gain control of the farm and then fight among them-selves. Orwell's pigs are Machiavellian creatures. Comrade Pig, on the other hand, is a friendly creature. Sloshing about in the mud, he watches the captain's activities with pleasure, and the captain is quite fond of him and knows that enjoying the mud is the pig's business.

†Charles Chaplin has a similar scene in *The Gold Rush.* Charles Chaplin. He was progressive. Clarice Lispector also describes a hen being chased in her short story *The Hen.*

meat diet retrograde, although he wasn't absolutely sure that this was indeed the case.

In fifteen days, New Birobidjan began to take shape: The vegetable garden had been planted; the comrade animals had a shelter. The site of the future power plant, whose gigantic turbines would supply energy to the tractor factory, had already been demarcated. The Palace of Culture was temporarily housed in a small lean-to. In the evenings the captain would read passages from Rosa Luxemburg's writings. On Thursdays the Festival of the Progressive Arts was held, the drawings in the album were exhibited, and Birobidjan recited Mayakovsky:

> *"To the barricades!*
> *I say:*
> *to the barricades of the soul and the heart!"*

Walt Whitman:

> *"Pioneers! O pioneers!*
> *All the past we leave behind,*
> *We debouch upon a newer mightier world, varied world,*
> *Fresh and strong the world we seize, world of labor and*
> *the march,*
> *Pioneers! O pioneers!"*

In addition, he read Isaac Babel's short stories.

Isaac Babel, from Odessa, was the son of a Jewish merchant. After the Russian Revolution he rode with Budenny's cavalry as a political commissar. He wrote short stories based on his war experiences. Later he was arrested and sent to a concentration camp, where he died in 1941. In 1942 Captain Birobidjan had no knowledge of this fact, and neither did anyone else. It wasn't until 1956, when the striking disclosures about the Stalin era were made, that this fact was to come to light.

Birobidjan particularly liked a short story titled *Salt*. A woman, a reactionary, boards a train with a sack of salt (destined for the black market); she tries to trick a soldier called Nikita Balmashev into believing that she is carrying a child in the sack. When her ruse is exposed, she says: "You're not really concerned about Russia. All you want is to help those filthy Jews, Lenin and Trotsky." Overcome by justifiable indignation, Nikita Balmashev executes the counterrevolutionary, saying: "We'll treat all traitors ruthlessly." Whenever Captain Birobidjan got to this point in the story, he would raise his voice and fix his eyes on Comrade Hen, hoping that she would take the hint. She pretended to be pecking away at the ground. How shameless could one be!

The captain spent the evenings producing an edition of *The Voice of New Birobidjan*. This handwritten newspaper had a circulation of one single copy. On Sunday evenings the captain would read it aloud to the comrades, and afterward post it on the bulletin board in the Palace of Culture. The masthead displayed the symbol of New Birobidjan—the letters *N* and *B* intertwined with a plow, a hoe, a power lathe, a painter's palette, a telescope, a book, and a test tube; beneath this drawing, the historical sentence: "We are now beginning the building of a new society." The editorial consisted of a proclamation addressed to Comrade Pig, Comrade Goat and—in particular—Comrade Hen, urging them to increase productivity. It was followed by a comentary on the international situation; Birobidjan reported that the Republicans in Spain had gained some major victories—in 1942! It was a lie, but how could he admit defeat? How could he admit that notwithstanding the heroic battle cry—*"No pasarán!"* the Fascists had indeed passed? How could he allow defeatism to overcome the comrade animals? Wouldn't this merely bring about disastrous consequences for New Birobidjan—such as, for example, Comrade Goat yielding less milk?

He would rather lie. Birobidjan knew that one progressive lie was worth more than the entire reactionary truth. Therefore, he described the magnificent victories in Madrid, in Bilbao.

Next came a transcription of Rosa Luxemburg's *Letters from Prison,* illustrated with a drawing showing the pure, lit-up face of the immortal Rosa. The captain was now able to recall in detail the features of that revered face, which as a matter of fact, became a recurrent motif in his all his drawings.

The news about New Birobidjan was enthusiastic: "The corn crop, the biggest ever, will exceed all expectations!" The progressive corn plants. "The bean plants are sprouting vigorously, as never before!" The loyal bean plants. There were congratulations on Comrade Hen's birthday ... Deep down in his heart the captain was a sentimentalist; he himself acknowledged that he was. If he had to use one hand to strike someone, he would always find a way of caressing with the other. Besides, he hoped that this incentive would bring Comrade Hen to her senses and integrate her with the production process. He really didn't want to drag her to the bar of the People's Tribunal, where conviction would be inevitable.

The newspaper also had a leisure section consisting of quizzes and crossword puzzles; the captain allowed himself this small indulgence, for he enjoyed such innocent forms of recreation. Even so, this undertaking was meant to sharpen his own recollection of important ideological topics. Who was "the great philosopher, a friend of Marx's, the author of *Anti-Dühring*," six letters? Engels, of course. For how could anyone forget about Engels? How could anyone forget that he was born in Barmen, Germany, in 1820, and died in 1895? Engels.

1942 came to an end. The captain entered 1943 lying in his tent, listening to the rain drumming on the canvas. Once more he missed his home, especially the children and the hot soup that Léia made on rainy nights. He felt like crying, but choked back his tears. He didn't want the comrade animals to witness the depressing display of his weakness. He spent the remainder of New Year's Eve stifling his sobs.

He woke up quite late. A summer sun warmed New Birobidjan. Ashamed, he crawled out of the tent, walked past the comrade animals, heading for the creek, there to wash up. A surprise awaited him by the Palace of Culture: Comrade Hen had laid an egg. Birobidjan lets out a whoop of joy: His ideological work has finally paid off!

Quickly, he gets hold of the egg. It's still warm. For weeks now Birobidjan has lived on nothing but vegetables and the scanty provisions he gets from the food store.

All of a sudden he is overcome by qualms: Is he entitled to the egg? Isn't it common property? Birobidjan sits down in anguish. One egg ... Not enough for the four of them, yet quite enough for himself; however, he can't seize it just like that. Besides, he will be guilt-ridden if he eats it before he starts his workday. And then an idea strikes him, an idea that makes him laugh and clap his hands, an idea that convinces him that his mission in life is to provide leadership. Climbing up onto a rock, he demands silence and then announces that he is going to make a statement. In the new year, he says, efforts must be redoubled. Right now, he announces, there is a prize to be given to the comrade that works the hardest in the vegetable garden: an egg. The contest begins right away: Birobidjan breaks into a run and throws himself into the task of weeding; he sings and strikes the earth with the hoe ... One egg! He'll have it for lunch. He might even make some soup!

And then he sees a woman standing by the flagpole.
"Léia!"
He goes running to her, embraces and kisses her, weeping.
"How are the children, Léia? And how did you find me?"
They sit down by the flagpole. Birobidjan notices that his wife

has grown thin; her eyes blink more often than they used to; and when she tries to light a cigarette, she can't; her hands shake too much.

"You smoking now, Léia? You, smoking?"

"And what did you expect?"

They look at each other. She sees a strange creature before her, a suntanned man with a long beard, who stares at her with glittering eyes.

"And the children, how are they?"

"Fine ..."

She wipes her eyes.

"Don't cry, Léia. I'm all right, can't see you I am? I've never felt so good, I eat well ..."

"Do you?" She studies him carefully. "But you're so skinny, Mayer!"

"No, I just got rid of all those rolls of fat. Look, I'm all muscle now! I eat well ..."

"Do you really?"

"Of course I do. Today, for instance, I'm having soup for lunch. The soup is just like the one you used to make. And there'll be an egg too, except that I haven't decided yet whether I'll have it fried or boiled ..."

"Boiled. Fried eggs don't agree with you."

"That's true!" the captain says with a laugh. "That's true, Léia. I had forgotten that fried eggs don't agree with me, but you haven't, isn't that so, Léia? You always think of me! And how are the children?"

"They're fine ..." Léia looks around. "Where do you live? In the house?"

"You remember this house, don't you, Léia? Remember that night, Léia?"

"Do you live there?"

"No ... I decided I'd live in a tent. It's cooler, especially now in the summer."

"And what about the cold nights? Or when it rains?"

"The tent is quite cozy, Léia, honest! And the rain doesn't get into it."

She seems rather skeptical. She opens her bag: "Thought I'd bring you a few things."

The captain sees a pullover, woolen socks, bread, oranges, three onions.

"Thanks, Léia, but I don't really need anything . . . as you can see, today, for example, there's so much to choose from that I haven't even made up my mind yet about what I'll have . . . Soup, egg . . . Thanks, anyhow. When I want to have something different to eat . . . And Spartacus?"

"Who?" She knits her brows.

"Jorge . . . Do you still read *The Pirates' Book* aloud to him? That passage that says: 'The Portuguese sailor lies afloat, motionless, half-drowned . . .' Do you?"

"That's right!" Léia smiles, surprised. "So, you do remember, Mayer, don't you? You haven't forgotten us, Mayer."

"There's something I'd like to tell you." Birobidjan looks serious. "You shouldn't be reading such books to our children. They have no educational value. You should read them Babel's short stories. Babel writes well, he's progressive, he . . ."

Mayer stops talking. For a while they remain silent.

"Remember that day when we first came here?" the captain asks. "Remember how you sneaked into my room, quite noiselessly? And remember Marc Friedmann the next day?" He imitates Marc's effeminate tone of voice: " 'I don't think it's fair. It's not fair . . .' "

Léia smiles timidly. "Ah, well, Mayer . . . pipe dreams, that's what they were . . ."

The captain gets to his feet.

"No, Léia, they weren't pipe dreams. We had an ideal, Léia, a great ideal, which I'm now putting into practice. Come, I'll show you around."

He shows her the vegetable garden, the site of the future power plant, the pole with the flag, the Palace of Culture. When they get to the tent, the captain can't resist the impulse to hug her tenderly.

"Léia ..."

They enter the tent. The captain is imbued with the ardor of a pioneer and Léia responds to it, moaning and sighing with pleasure. Then all of a sudden, she lets out a scream: "Someone has licked me!"

The captain jumps to his feet.

"An animal! It licked my foot!"

Birobidjan lifts a corner of the canvas. He sees Comrade Goat.

"It's Comrade Goat," he says, laughing.

"Who?" Léia looks about suspiciously.

"Comrade Goat," the captain repeats. "She has the best milk in the world, right Comrade Goat?"

He hugs the animal, murmuring terms of endearment. "It's Comrade Goat, my darling pretty one ..." Léia averts her eyes.

Later they go for a walk in the woods. Léia tries to persuade him to go back to Bom Fim.

"You're wasting your breath, Léia. Can't you understand? We're beginning the building of a new society here."

Now it is the captain's turn to try to persuade her to move to New Birobidjan, together with the children.

"We'll lead a healthy life here, free from oppression."

"Oh, yes," she says sarcastically, "free from oppression and in the company of animals. Comrade Goat and God knows who else ..."

"Comrade Hen and Comrade Pig," adds the captain.

"Comrade Hen, Comrade Pig, indeed!" She looks at him, almost frightened. "You're not right in your head, Mayer."

"I'll agree with any reservations you might have about Comrade Hen," he says, seriously. "I myself have criticized her sev-

58

eral times. As for Comrade Pig, he's loyal and brave. If he doesn't work hard that's due to his nature . . ."

"Do you really think I would throw the children into this zoo you have here?" Léia is losing her patience. "Besides, you don't own this place. It belongs to Marc Friedmann. Just wait until he finds out about this."

"The land belongs to whomever cultivates it!" shouts Birobidjan. Out of the corner of his eye he sees the little men hiding behind a bush and smiling at him.

Léia is now sobbing. Birobidjan tries to comfort her, but she rebuffs him. She looks at her watch. "I have to go home, but first I'll cook lunch for you."

She walks toward Birobidjan's makeshift kitchen. Embarrassed, he follows her: "You don't have to, Léia . . ."

She's already rummaging about the flatware, the pots and pans, muttering, "There's a shortage of just about everything here. Well, well . . ." Birobidjan lights the kitchen fire. After a while she succeeds in producing a salad, soup, and rice with egg. The captain looks at the plate, cheerlessly.

"This egg, Léia . . ."

"What's wrong with it?"

"I wanted to cook it myself. You see, it was a prize that I earned . . ."

"What prize? It was an egg just like any other. Eat."

"No, Léia . . ."

"Eat."

"I wouldn't enjoy it."

"Eat. I have to leave in a moment."

"Léia . . ."

"Eat! Eat! Eat!"

In desperation, she bites her wrists, tears her hair, and howls like a wounded goat. Frightened, Birobidjan bolts down the food. Léia bursts into tears, her head hidden in her hands.

When the captain finishes eating, she gets up, picks up her things, and without saying a word, walks toward the gate. Birobidjan heaves a sigh, picks up the hoe, and sets about working in his garden.

☆☆

1943

THE CAPTAIN HAD ALWAYS BEEN UNDER THE IMPRESsion that Marc Friedmann's hobby farm had been abandoned and that nobody lived there. He was wrong.

Four men and a woman lived in a wooden shack on the edge of the property. The men were ragpickers. They were always dirty and hungry. They liked to joke: They would tell the woman that if they had three other buddies they would be like Snow White and the Seven Dwarfs. They would leave the shack in the morning but wouldn't go very far; they would sit in the sun and spend hours drinking, talking, and playing cards. Since they were good friends, theirs was a pleasant, noncompetitive group. Their names were: Libório, Nandinho, Hortensio, and Fuinha. Libório sometimes enjoyed fishing in the river and Nandinho rather liked to explore the surrounding areas in search of stray chickens. Hortensio, skillful at the slingshot, would kill a bird every now and then. Fuinha was good at recognizing the value of certain herbs.

The woman never said much. She cooked, tidied the shack as well as she could, and tried to cultivate the land, but with no success because Libório would always trample on the corn plants as soon as they began to sprout. At night, she would lie down with all four of them. Her position would vary: sometimes on the corner, either facing Libório or with her back turned to him; sometimes between Libório and Nandinho, with her back turned to Libório and facing Nandinho; sometimes between Nandinho and Hortensio, facing Nandinho and with her back to Hortensio; sometimes with her back to Nandinho and facing Hortensio, and so forth.

Their shack consisted of one single room; there was no electricity, no running water, no drainpipes, no wooden floor, no windows, no shelves on which to put books. And yet it was picturesque: Located on the top of a small hill, it overlooked a field covered with bromeliads.

Hortensio had a big scar on his face. Fuinha had Indian features. Nandinho was constantly singing softly, and Libório had a beard. They had only one coat among them; in winter they wrapped themselves in sackcloth and their teeth chattered. On such occasions Libório would murmur: "What a wretched life, my friends. It's the pits!" Then he would burst into tears and cry for a long time.

Sometimes they would take a walk around the hobby farm and have a look at the house, but they never got really close to it for they believed it to be haunted.

It was during one of these walks that they first saw Captain Birobidjan. It was a beautiful day; the captain was working in his vegetable garden, weeding and singing. The four of them were quite startled to see him and hid themselves behind a clump of bamboo, from where they stood watching him.

"It's the owner," said Libório.

"Couldn't be. The owner never sets foot here," Nandinho said.

"Maybe it's a ghost," said Hortensio.

"Ghost my ass," Fuinha sneered. "Who has ever heard of a ghost weeding?"

When they saw the captain talking to the animals, they came to the conclusion that the man must be nuts. Later they witnessed the ceremonial lowering of the flag and the reading of poems by the light of the campfire. The captain ate dinner, washed the dishes, and crawled into the tent.

Libório, Nandinho, Hortensio, and Fuinha were pranksters. That night they began a series of practical jokes on Captain Birobidjan.

On the *first night* they repeatedly lifted a corner of the tent, pulled Captain Birobidjan's toes, and then broke into a run. At first, Captain Birobidjan thought it was the work of Comrade Goat and he laughed; then it dawned on him that Comrade Goat *licked* but didn't *pull*. Every time this happened, he would get up and step outside; by moonlight he would scrutinize the fields, the planted land, the clump of bamboo rustling in the wind. Nothing. He would go back to the tent and fall asleep. A moment later, it started all over again ... And so it went until dawn.

On the *second night* they placed a nutria, which they had caught in the marsh, inside the tent. Birobidjan was gripped by an overwhelming fear.

On the *third night* it was a small snake, with the same results.

On the *fourth night* they placed two large hairy spiders near the captain's pillow; then the four friends tried to visualize the position of the spiders.

"They're now near his face," said Libório.

"They're about to climb on his neck," Nandinho conjectured.

"No, only one of them is climbing on his neck; the other one is climbing on his face," Hortensio contradicted.

"How would you know?" Fuinha was annoyed. "It could well be that one of the spiders wants to enter his mouth."

"So what?" Hortensio said with growing irritation. "It can't enter his mouth unless it walks on his face first."

A frightening scream cut short this argument. By the moonlight they could see the captain running at full career across the fields.

On the *fifth night* the captain couldn't even eat any dinner. He was so drowsy that all he could do was stagger all day amid the corn plants; as soon as the sun went down, he got into the tent and immediately fell asleep. When the four friends heard him snoring, they rubbed their hands in glee. They had prepared their best prank yet for that night . . .

At around eleven o'clock the captain was having a nightmare. He was dreaming that he was working in a quarry and that he had to quarry a ton of granite per hour. The owner had pulled a gun on him: "Damn you! Keep working, you proletarian pig!" Suddenly a boulder came rolling down and landed smack on his chest, throwing him to the ground, where he lay buried, half-crushed . . .

He woke up running with sweat. With a great effort he managed to lift his head: There was a big stone lying on his chest! "So it wasn't a dream!" moaned the captain. He grabbed the stone with both hands and hurled it out of the tent.

There was a string: One end was secured to the stone; the other end was tied in a slipknot—around the captain's penis.

This time the scream was far louder than on any of the preceding nights. In the clump of bamboo, the four friends kept pummeling each other playfully and bursting into laughter. "I'll bet that was enough to yank his prick out!" Fuinha shouted. "I'll bet fifty thousand cruzeiros, wanna bet, anybody?" Nobody did; amid peals of laughter, they all agreed that it must have been. "For sure. No doubt about it!"

Their laughter gave them away. Quietly—his movements hindered by pain—the captain crawled toward the clump of bamboo. The four of them were discussing their plans for the following night. Nandinho suggested that they wrap the captain in the tent and throw him into the creek; Libório, however, wanted to strew his sleeping bag with live fish: "Live fish, think of it!

That would drive him nuts!" But Nandinho, who was drunk, muttered: "What I'd really like to do is to slit his throat and then take his tent, his pots and pans, his pig, everything." They argued for a while longer and then went away.

Birobidjan remained lying on the damp grass. Every so often he moaned, not because he was afraid but because he was in pain and enraged. *"No pasarán!"* he kept moaning.

1943. Stalingrad was putting up resistance. The Nazis were forced to retreat. Soon the Allies would be landing on the shores of Normandy ... 1943.

That very same night the captain called a meeting of the Defense Committee.

"Comrades," he began, "New Birobidjan is going through some difficult moments ..."

He paused. He pressed his lips together. Comrade Pig, Comrade Goat, and the little men were listening attentively, but Comrade Hen, as usual, was cackling frivolously. The captain looked hard at her.

"Comrades! The enemy have surrounded us. The enemy are powerful and ruthless. The enemy mean business, although there are some people who might think otherwise ..."

He looked at Comrade Hen again.

"Their goal is to destroy us. We must defend ourselves, comrades ..."

He interrupted himself dramatically, and looked at the comrades. Even Comrade Hen fell silent.

"I proclaim myself the generalissimo of New Birobidjan's armed forces!"

The little men applauded for a long time. The captain waited until the applause subsided and then went on: "From now our economy becomes a wartime economy. There'll be no superfluous expenditure. Our productivity must be increased. We must go to great pains to achieve this aim. If necessary we'll work twenty-four hours a day, but we will win the battle!"

65

The little men broke into applause again; Comrade Goat bleated; Comrade Pig grunted. When some manifestation was expected from Comrade Hen, she remained silent. This detail was not lost on the captain.

Birobidjan lit a fire, and although it was nighttime, he presided at the ceremony of the raising of the flag, after which he clamored once more for the comrades' participation in the fight. Then he adjourned the meeting. He wanted to be alone so that he could work out a defense plan.

On the following day he worked in the vegetable garden as usual. To maintain a semblance of normality in New Birobidjan was part of his tactics. In the evening he lowered the flag and put out the fire.

The attack took place soon after midnight. It had been raining, but the wind had dispersed the clouds and there was now a full moon. The enemy left the clump of bamboo; their arrogance was obvious; there were bursts of laughter, jeering remarks, insults. They were so convinced of the superiority of their forces that they had even gotten drunk.

Hidden in the bushes, the captain waited, full of confidence in his people's militia.

The enemy approach, singing songs full of mockery:

> "Let's have some soap, soap,
> Made from a fat little Jew . . ."

Fat! Looking at his thin arms, the captain smiles. The four men are advancing along the narrow trail . . .

With a scream, Libório disappears into the ground. He has fallen into the first trap, a deep ditch disguised with a flimsy cover made of twigs and leaves.

"There goes the first one!" murmurs the captain excitedly.

Instead of helping out their companion, the other three broke into a run; it was then that Nandinho fell into the second trap, and as he did so, he triggered a bamboo contrivance, which shot an arrow that nearly tore his ear away.* Hortensio and Fuinha beat a retreat. All of a sudden, Comrade Goat stepped out of the dense underbrush and went in hot pursuit of them, finally succeeding in butting Hortensio to the ground.

"Bravo!" shouted the captain. "Take heart, Comrade Goat!"

Running continuously, Fuinha ended up falling into the grassy marsh, where he sank into the mud.†

It was an out-and-out victory. Captain Birobidjan and his comrades got together for a joyous, friendly celebration, during which the captain sang "El Ejército del Ebro" and "Kalinka." Comrade Hen was nowhere to be found.

A victory rally was held the following day. Reporting on the event, *The Voice of New Birobidjan* stated the following:

> The rally was preceded by a great parade of workers, headed by Comrade Pig. He was followed by Comrade Goat, with the flag of New Birobidjan tied to her horns. As they walked past the dignitaries' platform, they were greeted by Comrade Mayer.
>
> Comrade Hen's defection must be mentioned. When invited to participate in the parade, she demonstrated her vacillation by cackling nervously. Finally, she flew away and perched herself in a tree. Her disgraceful behavior was witnessed by all present.
>
> In his speech, Comrade Mayer stressed the significance of this victory and congratulated

---

* Many years later, the Vietcong were to use a similar device against the North American troops. The Vietcong.

† A similar instance provided the theme for a passage in Prokofiev's cantata *Alexander Nevsky,* which celebrates the victory that the Russians, led by Prince Alexander Nevsky, gained over the Teutonic knights (12th century). The invaders fell into the icy waters of a lake rather than into a grassy marsh. The outcome, however, was identical in both cases. Alexander Nevsky.

everyone that took part in the parade; however,
he went on to deplore Comrade Hen's reactionary
behavior; her repeated omissions had indeed
cast her outside History. Mayer stated that the
Defense Committee had been contemplating
taking Comrade Hen before the People's Tribunal; however, such drastic measures have not
been taken yet due to Comrade Mayer's bene-
volence. The people applauded his speech for a
long time.

The festivities, which continued through the evening, culmi-
nated in a victory banquet. Birobidjan would dearly have liked
to have Comrade Hen as the main course—beheaded, plucked,
broiled, lying on her back on a platter, her legs sticking up, glis-
tening with juices. But he lost his nerve and opted for vegetables instead. And there was corn and beans and lettuce ... aplenty.
And wine as well; a bottle that the captain had saved for a
special occasion. He sang and recited poetry, always applauded
by the little men. Finally, he went to bed.

Before falling asleep, he thought of how he would try to find
the four men on the following day. They were not really wicked.
They were men of the people, and the people are always good.
Ignorant and crude, yes—yet human beings. He would reach
out to them. They would respond—and why shouldn't they? The
captain would invite them to visit New Birobidjan; they would
feel excited about the planted land, the site of the future power
plant, the Palace of Culture. And they would adjust themselves to New Birobidjan. They would, of course, have to go
through a period of indoctrination; the Political Committee
would see to it. Later they would integrate themselves into the
production process. There wouldn't be any problems. Historical determinism ...

His eyes closed. Silence fell upon New Birobidjan; everybody
was asleep, including the little men.

It was a mistake. It was a historical mistake. Captain Birobidjan had underestimated the forces of reaction.

He woke up coughing and feeling suffocated. The tent was on fire! Grabbing his clothes, the captain crawled outside.

New Birobidjan was on fire. Everything was ablaze: the cornfield, the comrade animals' house, the Palace of Culture, everything one single gigantic bonfire.

Without realizing what he was doing, the captain began to run across the fields. The bromeliads pricked his naked feet cruelly, but he didn't stop to put on his boots. He arrived at the house, hurled himself against the door, which yielded against his weight and flew open. Captain Birobidjan rolled on the dusty floor. And there he remained, lying on the floor. He was weeping. He was weeping the way his grandfather had wept after the pogrom in Kishinev: crying out and beating his breast with his clenched fist. He wept over the settlement now burned to the ground, over the cultivated land, over the Palace of Culture, over the pole and its flag. He wept over the millions of workers scattered all over the world; thin people with pallid faces, whose huge eyes no longer shed tears.

He lay weeping for a long time.

Then gradually he calmed down. He got up and bolted the door. Wiping his tears, he tried to assess the situation. He walked through the house, striking matches so that he could examine it. The floor was strewn with dead animals: mice, spiders, insects. The captain had to step on the poor shriveled bodies. He bolted all the doors and went back to the living room; only then did he realize that he was wearing nothing but his underpants. He got dressed. Then, holding a piece of rusty pipe, he sat down on the only piece of furniture left in the house, the brown leather couch, which was placed in front of a window. He didn't dare close the wooden shutters; there was a faint light filtering through the windows.

He was afraid of . . . the dark. Yes, of the dark.

Hours went by. The captain kept nodding off. Suddenly he opened his eyes, startled, feeling that he was being watched. A few minutes later, fragments of glass were flying all over and something came rolling across the floor and then halted at his feet. The captain struck a match.

It was Comrade Pig's bleeding head. Not long after, Comrade Goat's head also came rolling across the floor.

The captain couldn't contain a sob. Crawling across the floor, he reached the window and bolted the shutters. Then he went back to where the heads were lying. By the light of matches he stood gazing at them for a long time. He wanted to tell them that their sacrifice hadn't been in vain; he wanted to tell them that they had sown the seeds of a better world—but he couldn't. He merely mumbled farewell.

He heard voices outside. Peeping through the keyhole, he saw the four men and a woman. They stood around a big fire, over which they were broiling chunks of Comrade Pig and Comrade Goat. They were passing a bottle.

It was the barbecue ceremony, which Birobidjan had always commended to the comrades—an authentic popular tradition, he used to say, to be preserved in the new society. Now, however, it merely filled him with sadness and loathing.

Then an argument broke out among the men. Apparently, two of them wanted to leave, while the other two wanted to stay. The woman was trying to conciliate. Finally, one of the men staggered forward and stopped close to the house.

"Come out, you bastard!" he shouted. "Come out if you're enough of a man, you coward! Why don't you come and fight with us? Open this door and step outside!"

The woman tried to hold him back; he pushed her away. Then she picked up a piece of firewood and hit him on the back.

A moment later all four of them were on top of the woman,

pummeling her, biting her, trampling upon her. When they finally stopped, she lay lifeless. They picked her up, holding her by the legs and arms. Terror-stricken, Birobidjan saw that they were heading for the door.

"It's a battering ram!"

A battering ram. The Romans had used it for breaking through the doors of the towns that resisted their imperialist onslaughts.

There was a thud on the door—followed by another, and yet another. Birobidjan entrenched himself behind the couch. Gripping the piece of pipe in his hand, he stood waiting, his teeth clenched, his forehead moist with sweat.

"*No pasarán!*" he kept murmuring. "*No pasarán!*"

The thudding stopped.

"Let's leave her here. Come on, let's go."

Then there was silence. Birobidjan waited for a few minutes and then went to the door. He peeped through the keyhole and saw the men already in the distance. Could it be a trap? He hesitated.

Finally, he unbolted the door and opened it. The first thing he saw was the woman, who was lying on the front yard. Blood was oozing from her forehead. The captain went over and touched her with his fingertips: She was warm. She was alive. Pretty beaten-up, but alive. The captain got some water and washed her face. The woman stirred and moaned.

"You've cracked my head open, you faggots!"

Birobidjan dragged her indoors. He lay her on the couch; then he threw himself upon the floor and fell asleep.

He woke up, startled. From the couch the woman was watching him with interest. She was still young; her features were coarse and her face was freckled, but her eyes were a deep blue.

"What's your name?" the captain asked.

"Santinha . . . Did you rescue me from those thugs, mister . . .?"

"Don't call me 'mister,'" said the captain, pulling on his boots.

71

"What shall I call you then?"

" 'Comrade.' Yes, I did rescue you."

"Comrade?"

"That's right. Comrade Mayer. Do you live around here?"

"Yeah, I mean, not here in the house. Near the fence."

"Good." The captain got to his feet. It was important to show resoluteness, he well knew; after all, he wasn't absolutely sure that she wasn't one of the enemy. "What did you say your name was?"

"Santinha."

"I don't like it. It's a reactionary name. I'll call you Rosa Luxemburg."

"Rosa what?"

"Luxemburg. Haven't you heard about her? She founded the Spartacus Party."

"Never heard of either," said the woman, with suspicion. "I'm new around here. I'm from Santa Catarina. Anyhow, if you, mister ..."

"Comrade."

"Okay. If you, comrade, think that it's a good name, we're not going to quarrel over it, right? What's that name again?"

"Rosa Luxemburg."

"I won't forget it." She let out a moan of pain. "Oh, what a splitting headache!"

The captain opened the door.

"It must be about ten o'clock," he said. "I'm hungry."

He regretted having said so. He should have shown himself as being strong, immune to hunger.

"Is there anything to eat in this house?" she asked.

"No."

She stood thinking for a while. Then she gave a little laugh. "I have all their money. I'll go to the store and get us some coffee, milk, bread, and lots of goodies. We'll eat well. That'll teach those bastards a lesson."

She got up. As he watched her walk away, the captain was thinking that a new era was about to arise in New Birobidjan. He would have to establish a new settlement—in the territory surrounding the house, seeing that the old location had proved insecure. Walking about outside, the captain began to designate the sites of the cultivated land, of the future power plant, of the Palace of Culture, and also—Birobidjan heaved a sigh—of the Heroes' Mausoleum, where the skulls of Comrade Pig and Comrade Goat would rest. And where was Comrade Hen? The captain knitted his brow. She must have sold out to the enemy.

Rosa Luxemburg would help him. She would have to go through a period of indoctrination, of course; the Political Committee would see to it. Maybe now was the time to found the People's University of New Birobidjan ... He would be responsible for teaching the classes. It would add to his load, but it would prevent the university from being subject to deviations (such as the slackening of revolutionary discipline, the formation of splinter groups opposing party policies, and so forth). Rosa Luxemburg—Comrade Rosa. The captain thought of a drawing for his album (which fortunately, as he was to find out later, hadn't been damaged in the blaze): Himself, marching along a road, his face illuminated by the rays of the sun, his left hand holding a rifle, his right hand signaling to Rosa Luxemburg to follow him, which she does with a calm, trusting smile.

Lying on the grass in the hot sun, Birobidjan devises a strategy plan. In the end everything will turn out all right, in accordance with historical determinism. In the future Rosa might even be asked to join the Central Committee—optimistically, he comes to this conclusion.

However, how would he relate to her? A difficult problem. Before the masses, of course, they would be merely the Comrade Leaders. But when they were in his office? What would happen in the course of those extended meetings? After they had exhausted the political and economic subjects, and she started

talking about personal feelings? When his hand would unin-
tentionally brush against her arm? When her eyes sparkled?

Rosa Luxemburg returned, loaded with groceries.

"I got the food!" she shouted from a distance. "There's plenty
of stuff for the two of us!"

She crouched down by the captain and started to gather kin-
dling to make a fire.

The captain pulled her toward him. It was the beginning of
love, this pure revolutionary emotion.

Meanwhile in Bom Fim, Mayer Guinzburg had become the
talk of the streets. He was the favorite conversation topic not only
of the women shopping up and down Rua Felipe Camarão but
also of the men gathered in front of the Serafim on Sunday
mornings.

They tell shocking stories about him. They say that he dresses
in rags; that he has grown a beard; that he eats nothing but
pork. Leib Kirschblum adds that Mayer Guinzburg lives in what
looks like a fortress; above his bed there is a portrait of Stalin,
before which Mayer kneels every morning, shouting: "Stalin, my
leader, my god! Fill me with inspiration! Guide me along your
path! Embrace me, give me your warmth!" and other things like
that.

When questioned about Mayer, José Goldman defends his
friend. "His behavior is consistent with his ideas," he explains;
however, he would much rather stay out of the discussions. "Do
you think he's crazy?" he asks his wife over lunch. "Forget about
him," she replies, "and eat."

Some women are outraged and demand that their husbands
do something about him.

"He's killing his wife and children!"

Leib Kirschblum decides to have a word with Marc Friedmann,
who lives in an apartment on Rua Duque de Caxias, quite a
long way from Bom Fim. He finds him at home; he is wearing

a robe and talking to a youth with a dark complexion. Leib
Kirschblum informs him about what has been going on in his
property in Beco do Salso; he gives him a detailed account of
Mayer Guinzburg's degeneration; he concludes by requesting that
Marc do something about this situation. Marc Friedmann breaks
into laughter.

"That Mayer! He's always been so crazy, so impulsive ... Deep
in my heart I do like him."

"But he's squatting on your land ..." reasons Leib Kirschblum.

"Oh, let him," replies Marc. "I don't mind. I think it's rather
romantic ..."

Leib Kirschblum returns to Bom Fim foaming at the mouth.

"I've wasted my breath talking to that faggot," he remarks to
his friends. He decides to set up a committee to talk to Mayer.
They'll appeal to whatever remains of his Jewish feelings; they'll
show him old Guinzburg's book of prayers; they'll cry out: "It's
the spirit of Israel that asks you to return home!" They'll reason
with him. They'll threaten him. Everybody will praise Leib's
acumen. Which will suit him fine, for he's thinking of running
for the presidency of the Israelite Social Circle.

The captain illustrated the committee's visit in his album "The
One-Man Army." The *first drawing* depicts a group of men arriving in New Birobidjan: They are dressed in elegant clothes,
they smoke big cigars, they wear pearl pins on their neckties.
In their eyes one can see: *contempt, disgust, derision,* as well as a
certain *fear.*

In the *second drawing* Birobidjan appears. He stands behind the
people's podium; the wind ruffles his hair and his long beard.
His eyes glitter. With a pointing finger, he fulminates at the
bourgeoisie.

In the *third drawing* the dandies beat a retreat. In the background, the little workers laugh at them. They didn't allow
themselves to be defeated by the petit bourgeois attempts to black-
mail them; they showed strength, that's why they are so happy

now, singing and dancing. In this same drawing, Rosa Luxemburg's avenging finger indicates the exit to the undesirable visitors.

The committee returned to Bom Fim rather discouraged.

"It's a hopeless case," said Leib Kirschblum. "He has sold his soul to the Red devil."

Some of the others, however, were remarking—in a low voice—that Mayer Guinzburg was fending for himself quite nicely.

"He's even gotten himself a maid—and not bad-looking at all ..."

José Goldman was incensed at this fact.

"A maid! He has sold out to the bourgeoisie!"

Leib Kirshblum went to the store to break the news to Léia. She listened to him in silence, while folding shirts on a counter. Léia and Leib Kirschblum's wife were cousins and he felt responsible for her: "I'll start a collection to help you out ... You can't expect anything from him. The Reds are heartless."

Léia kept on folding the shirts in silence.

The captain laughed a great deal after the committee's visit; as a matter of fact, he had good reason for his merriment. Rosa Luxemburg had proved herself to be an active proletarian. She had cleaned up the entire house; had improvised a bed, using canvas and dried hay; had made a stove from stones and a discarded grate. She had cut down a eucalyptus tree, had lopped off all its branches and twigs, and then had erected it as a mast, ready to receive the flag of New Birobidjan, which the captain was in the process of making. She had started a corn patch and had demarcated the site for the future power plant.

And her work wasn't confined to the settlement. At dawn, she was already on her way to the streetcorners, where she hung around, either hawking or panhandling. She never came home empty-handed. The captain didn't starve and he even acquired new clothes—a tunic that had once been worn by a sergeant from the local brigade.

Birobidjan worked too, but without his former drive. He would hoe for a while and then would lie down; or he would spend hours at the Heroes' Mausoleum polishing the skulls of Comrade Pig and Comrade Goat, while cursing Comrade Hen under his breath. At times he would sing—but what he sang weren't always revolutionary songs; he now favored old Yiddish tunes.

The Voice of New Birobidjan was several issues behind; May Day came and went without even a mass rally to mark it; and it had been a long time since the Central Committee had held a meeting. Before Rosa Luxemburg, however, he would put on a façade of ideological vigor, a vigor he no longer possessed. He would say that their personal relationship must not affect the production relations; that it was important not to neglect the crops; that the enemy kept prowling about ...

"What enemy?" she would interject. "If you mean those bums, they've chucked me here and are gone. Kind of gypsy-like, they are."

The captain, however, kept on harping on the threat of extermination. He would wake her up in the night, saying he had heard noises; without her knowledge, he would draw strange symbols with charcoal on the outside walls of the house; he would claim that Indians lived in the area, and he would tell tales of massacres. He kept her in a constant state of anxiety, and he even devised a series of military exercises. Rosa had to crawl across swamps, climb trees, dig trenches; she learned how to make simple traps, where she would catch birds from the woods; under the captain's orders, she would kill them, pluck them, and eat them raw. "If you light a fire," he would explain, "the smoke might attract the enemy."

He proclaimed himself generalissimo. Rosa remodeled the old tunic, adding gold stripes, as befitted the high rank of his office. From then on the military maneuvers became even more strenuous than before.

Nevertheless, Rosa would have small outbursts of rebelliousness. Once the captain surprised her in the pantry, where she was devouring the entire extra supply of food. When he reprimanded her, reminding her that they were in a wartime economy, she replied, her mouth stuffed with bread, "But I'm hungry! I haven't had a square meal in days!"

He turned his back on her. From the couch, where he was now sitting, he overheard her muttering, "This tightfisted Jew wants to starve me to death! War, my ass! The war is over. I want to eat."

Birobidjan left the house and hid himself in the woods. That night he bivouacked on the site of the former settlement.

Rosa Luxemburg went in search of him, and tearfully asked for his forgiveness. To compromise, however, was out of the question: He did return home, but that night he handed her over to the People's Tribunal. He accused her in the most vehement terms; he gave her the opportunity to defend herself, which she refused. She was found guilty. The sentence in such cases was execution by shooting; however, it was changed—due to necessary adjustment to local conditions—to stoning to death.

Standing in the yard in front of the house, Rosa waited, trembling. Birobidjan had armed himself with pieces of brick; he was now taking aim at her, but then he remembered that stoning to death was an ancient Biblical punishment. He wouldn't do it.

I won't retrogress to centuries ago, he said to himself.

This weakness was possibly an error. Discipline began to slacken off. Rosa still worked as hard as usual, however her insolence kept growing. Birobidjan took a dim view of her behavior.

One day when the captain woke up—at nine o'clock in the morning—he saw, much to his surprise, that Rosa was still asleep. He shook her violently.

"I'm not going out today," she muttered.

"And why not?"

"It's Sunday. I won't be working on Sundays anymore."

"And why not?" Birobidjan was astonished.

"I'm Catholic. I'll spend Sundays praying."

"Very well," mocked the captain. "So, you'll go to heaven, but we'll starve to death."

She got up, furious.

"Don't you dare make fun of my religion, you Jew!"

"Who told you I'm a Jew?"

She laughed. "You think I haven't noticed your prick with the cut-off skin?"

"So what?" said Birobidjan, with contempt. "It's a superstitious practice. Done against my will. As a matter of fact, I'm am atheist."

Nervously, he began to pace to and fro; suddenly, he stopped and turned to her: "I now decree that there won't be any kind of religion whatsoever in New Birobidjan. Religion is the opium of the people. And this subject is now closed for good."

Rosa Luxemburg was stubborn. She didn't work that day. Then the captain decided it was time to strengthen his authority; he began to order her around more often than before, for the simple reason that he enjoyed doing so. He wouldn't let her eat until he had finished his meal, and then he wouldn't leave her much to eat. Finally, he demanded that she address him as "mister" and "sir."

"But why?" she asked, her eyes brimming with tears. "We've slept together, haven't we? How can I call you sir?"

Birobidjan felt sorry for her. "Okay, so call me . . ." He paused for a moment to turn the matter over in his mind. What form of address should he choose for himself? Chief? Chairman? Then an idea came into his mind: "Call me 'Captain.' Captain Birobidjan."

"Captain! That's it!" She broke into laughter and clapped her hands. "Beautiful! Captain! Oh, my little Captain!"

She was jumping for joy and singing:

> *"Cap, cap*
> *Mister Captain,*
> *a sword at the waist,*
> *leading a jennet by the hand."*

Birobidjan was laughing with her. She let herself fall on the floor, where she lay panting.

"Why 'Captain'?" she wanted to know.

"It's because . . ." He hesitated. "I was a captain once, didn't you know?"

"I didn't," she said in amazement. "I really know nothing about you. You never tell me anything. I don't even know where you come from, whether you're Brazilian or not . . . I've always thought you're nuts!"

"Shut up!" he said with growing irritation. "I told you I was a captain once. I was and I am. Captain Birobidjan. Birobidjan because that's the name of this place here. A new society will begin here."

"A club, is it?" She opened her eyes wide.

Birobidjan laughed. A moment later he was lying on top of her, kissing her furiously.

> *"That night I galloped*
> *along the best of roads . . ."**

It was the last time that he felt any real sexual pleasure. From then on he would make use of her as a matter of course—like a

---

*These lines were written by Lorca. Federico García Lorca: born in Spain in 1899. One of the most renowned individuals of his generation. Executed by shooting in 1936. Lorca.

farmer, he would say to himself, screwing his half-breeds. He would mount his tame mare and ride along the trails of tedium. And sometimes he would call her by her former name: "Santinha, come here!"

One day he took his album of drawings and walked toward the open country. Sitting in the shade of a tree, he considered going away and starting "The One-Man Army" all over again. But what would he draw? The portrait of a wild-eyed man with a long graying beard wearing a tattered tunic? What was this drawing supposed to depict? The leader of a group of pirates? An eccentric millionaire? A crazy rabbi?

He threw the pencil away. The little men were watching him in silence.

All of a sudden the captain realized what had been happening. It was nothing new: the exploitation of one class by another, the destruction of all values by brutal oppression. And who was the oppressor? He, Birobidjan. And who were the oppressed? Santinha, Rosa Luxemburg. Birobidjan got to his feet. He had found a way.

"She must rebel! It's impossible for this situation to persist! It's time to fight back! And if necessary, it'll be a bloody fight! Stand up, Comrade Rosa! You have nothing to lose except your fetters!"

The little men broke into applause.

"Free yourself, Rosa!" he repeated, and then, lowering his voice, "and free myself ... only you can do it!"

He ran toward New Birobidjan. He arrived home out of breath and went in through the back door.

"Rosa! Rosa!"

He found her in the bedroom with a bundle of clothes in her hands.

"Where are you going, Rosa?" he asked, surprised.

"My name is Santinha," she said in a flat tone of voice. "I'm leaving."

"But why?" Birobidjan grabbed her by the arm. "Why, Rosa?"

"Santinha. Because ... well, I think I might get a job working in a factory. It's better this way ... Captain."

"In a factory? But you'll be exploited in a factory!" Birobidjan shouted. "You're not going to surrender yourself, body and soul, to the bourgeoisie, are you?"

"Well, it's that ..." She sounded embarrassed. "They've come to take me with them."

"They who?"

"The four of them. All four of them."

Birobidjan opened the window. There they were, standing in the yard, near the flagpole on which someday the flag would be raised. They were amusing themselves by throwing their knives at the sapless trunk of the eucalyptus tree.

"Good-bye, Captain," said Rosa on her way out.

From the window the captain watched them walk away. Hortensio turned to shout, pointing to the flagpole: "If you need any comfort, there's a bottle near that stick of yours. Real good rum, comrade!"

The captain closed the window and threw himself on the bed. He was weeping. He was weeping the way his grandfather had wept after the pogrom in Kishinev; crying out and beating his chest with his clenched fist. He wept over New Birobidjan, over Rosa Luxemburg, who was returning to the condition of slavery; he wept over the millions of workers scattered all over the world, thin people with pallid faces, whose huge eyes had dried out after having wept so much. He wept over himself, over this poor, wretched Captain Birobidjan, who had once dreamed of a better world. He wept for a long time.

Gradually he calmed down. He got up, and went to the door. He gazed at the cultivated land, at the Palace of Culture (still bare), at the site of the future power plant, at the Heroes' Mausoleum. No! He wouldn't let New Birobidjan come to an end! He wouldn't surrender the settlement to reactionary forces! He would launch a new five-year plan. If necessary, he would work day and night—and single-handedly.

"There are many kinds of wars, comrades; in some we fight single-handedly!" he shouted. The little men applauded. The captain marched up to the flagpole, singing "El Ejército del Ebro." He hoisted the flag of New Birobidjan—no, of New New Birobidjan. The change of name would be symbolic of the new era. When the ceremony was over, the captain said in a hoarse voice: "We're now beginning the building of a new society."

It was then that his eyes fell upon the bottle. The captain wasn't given to indulging in vices; he would allow himself the odd chess game or crossword puzzle, and the occasional glass of wine, but he never drank rum, which he regarded as an opiumlike drug of the people. Nevertheless, he felt he would need a drink before launching his five-year plan. Afterward, he said to himself, everything will be solved. The bean plants will sprout, the corn plants will grow, the Palace of Culture will be in operation, *The Voice of New Birobidjan* will expound on doctrines, the power plant will generate electricity.

It wasn't long before the captain was drunk. He kept walking around and around the flagpole, challenging his enemies: "You, there! Yeah, you four bums! Come over here and fight if you're real men! Hello, Germans! Hello, Germans! Hello, Teutonic knights! Come over here and face Alexander Nevsky, the proletarian prince! Marc Friedmann, you faggot! Let's hear some self-criticism or I'll ram this flagpole up your ass! Leib Kirschblum, you poor bourgeois! If you think you're gonna take me back with you, you're dead wrong! Freud, you clown, you renegade Jew, you peddler of couches . . . of divans! And where's the owner of that quarry? Hey, where are you? Come here, you fink! Father, your Gemara is nothing but lies, do you hear me, Father?"

He began to knock down everything that stood in his path: the flagpole, the lean-to that housed the Palace of Culture, the

Heroes' Mausoleum. He kicked the skulls of Comrade Pig and Comrade Goat, sending them flying away. He entered the house and demolished the bed and the stove.

Then he went outside again. And all of a sudden he had an amazing vision: There in the yard stood Comrade Hen, calmly pecking at the ground. But she had grown huge, like Charles Chaplin's hen. The captain hesitated; then letting out his battle cry, *"No pasarán!"* he advanced upon her. She kept dodging him as Birobidjan pursued her, thinking that each of her thighs must yield at least a ton of meat.

"Don't try to escape, Comrade Hen! Fulfill your duty, you traitor! Offer your life as a sacrifice for the new society. Or would you rather face the People's Tribunal? Come here!"

He stumbled and rolled on the ground. Comrade Hen disappeared.

It was dawn when he woke up. A fog had enveloped everything: It was impossible for the captain to see the house, the woods, the trail, anything. It was like a sea. In this sea he was now afloat, motionless, half-drowned. He tried to raise himself but didn't succeed, so he drifted off to sleep again.

The sun revived him. He got up and, with difficulty, began to walk. He reached the road. He asked a tight-lipped drayman for a ride, then climbed onto his cart and settled himself among the sacks of vegetables.

"Can I have a carrot?" he asked. The man gestured affirmatively.

"But I can't pay you ..."

"That's all right," replied the drayman. "Help yourself."

They arrived at Bom Fim. Birobidjan alighted in front of the Serafim. People stared at the dirty, tattered creature and whispered.

Birobidjan walked to the store. He hesitated for a second before walking in.

At the counter, Léia stood folding shirts.

"Léia . . ."

Without a word, she closed the door, shutting out the onlookers. Then she walked through the curtain that separated the store from the house. He followed her.

The children were eating lunch. Upon seeing their father, Jorge started crying, but Raquel grinned and clapped her hands. Léia sent the children to the patio. Then she advanced upon him.

Mayor Guinzburg retreated abruptly. Léia pursued him throughout the house. In the *kitchen* she hit him with the *broom* and a *wooden spoon*; in the *bedroom*, she wielded a *pillow*; in the *bathroom* she succeeded in grabbing him and then she tried to push his head down into the *toilet*; in the *dining room* she flung *dishes, knickknacks, pictures*, a *candelabrum*, and a *samovar* at him. Finally, Mayer Guinzburg was on his knees, begging her for forgiveness. The children came in, weeping. Léia then hugged him; soon they were all hugging one another. The neighbors had forced the door open and were now pouring in; everybody was hugging everybody else, some were laughing and crying at the same time; others only crying. Leib Kirschblum, José Goldman, Avram Guinzburg, and even the cabbies from the taxi stand in the plaza! They greeted Mayer and Léia as if they were newlyweds. Then they began to leave.

Léia set the table. Mayer Guinzburg sat down and looked at the table laden with good, plentiful Yiddish food: The soup was just as he liked it, the *kneidlech* . . .

He picked up a spoon, then laid it down again. He felt like talking; he wanted to tell her all about New Birobidjan; about the comrade animals, the Palace of Culture, the cultivated land; about New Birobidjan . . .

"Eat," said Léia.

1944, 1945, 1946, 1947, 1948

"T HEN FOR SEVERAL YEARS," SAYS ARAM GUINZ-
burg, Mayer's brother, "he settled down. He worked in the store
and he worked really hard to provide for his family. It's true
that he didn't make much money ... but that's not a crime. He
became a good father, a good husband. It's a pity that Father
and Mother didn't live to see this transformation. They died soon
after the end of the war ... of a broken heart, I'd say, having
learned that the rest of our family in Europe had been killed in
a concentration camp. Mayer, too, grieved deeply. He really did,
I can assure you. As I said before, he was a different person. In
the daytime, he worked; in the evenings, he sat down with his
family, drank tea, and ate the strudel that Léia made especially
for him. He ate with appetite. We played cards ... At first he
didn't want to learn how to play, but then he changed his mind
and began to play with us. He was a good player."

His nephews and nieces were reconciled with him. Many years
later, when they learned that a book had been written about
him, they were surprised.

"A book about Uncle?" said the history professor. "I don't know

... True, there's a certain correlation between his own life and history, a correlation that imparts a certain transcendency to him; however, his life and history didn't always run parallel."

"It's a good book," remarked the librarian. "But I wish I had been consulted. The author looked up the facts in books, but the bibliographical references are totally inaccurate, not to mention that there are plenty of omissions. Why was there no mention made of the *Encyclopedia Britannica*? I'm sure that's where most of the data came from."

1944, 1945, 1946 ... Years. The war had ended. Mayer continued to work in the store. Seen from behind the counter, the days were always alike; in the dining room, the evenings were always alike: tea, strudel, card games, pleasant conversation. Time flowed into the vast sea, where Mayer Guinzburg lay afloat, motionless, half-drowned—like the Portuguese pirate in Antônio Barata's *The Pirates' Book*. The Portuguese sailor managed to escape from Campeche, where he had been imprisoned by the Spaniards. After traveling one hundred forty miles on foot, he reached Golfo Triste, where he found a community of pirates; they welcomed him, gave him a boat, and he set sail.

In 1948, at the time when the state of Israel was founded, he had moments of great emotion. Israel, where the collective farms kept multiplying. Where the building of a new society was under way. Enraptured, Mayer Guinzburg visualized dozens of flagpoles, of Palaces of Culture, of sites for future power plants. His eyes lost in the distance, he stood absentmindedly in the store until Léia admonished him.

Léia worked in the store as well, and she worked long hours. She would say to her customers: "There were even mice and cockroaches here. The cleanup was really hard work, but it was worthwhile."

"I'll bet it was," the customers would reply, looking at Mayer somewhat disapprovingly.

However, the fact was that business wasn't very good. The store couldn't compete with the big department stores, and Mayer was well aware of this fact. His income grew less every month. The children were demanding things. Jorge wanted a bicycle, all his friends had one.

"Buy books," Mayer would say. "Jorge Amado's, for instance."

"Books! Books! All you ever talk about is books! Why would I want books? To become a loony like you and run away to the woods?"

His son's defiance grieved Mayer. He was convinced that the boy suffered from some nervous disorder. He had read something about it; there was some new treatment for it, a treatment devised by Dr. Freud, who used a couch instead of pills.

Raquel was a dreamy girl. She would spend hours at the far end of the yard, talking to her doll. At the table, Léia would scold her, "Eat, Raquel!" Mayer, however, adored his daughter. She'll suffer deeply, he would say to himself. He wanted to shower her with gifts: dresses, new dolls, a little music box. Then he realized that he didn't make enough money. Leib Kirschblum owned a car; Avram had bought a house; and even José Goldman, he had heard, was well-off. He was the only one who remained poor. Léia didn't care for jewelry or clothes; she was, however, upset about not being able to take the children to the seaside.

"The sea is the source of all life," she would say with a sigh.

Many many years ago, the first forms of life began crawling with great difficulty out of the sea and onto the land, carrying inside them a small amount of the primeval liquid. Painfully, they became adjusted to aridity; but their nostalgia for the ocean persisted in the salinity of their own organic liquids, and in their secret yearnings for the gentle rocking of the waves. On some occasions, they found solace in the amniotic liquid in the uterus, or later, in the salty tears that they could taste in their mouths.

To return to the sea, therefore, was an everlasting longing, and year after year, the people of Bom Fim would head for the beaches of Capão da Canoa for their ceremonial bathing.

Mayer Guinzburg's family, however, had to be satisfied with the banks of the Guaíba River. Dejectedly, they splashed in its muddy waters, lukewarm like urine, while their neighbors enjoyed the invigorating Atlantic. Léia didn't complain, but she debited this fact, which was one more item on a growing list of debits, against her husband's account. Someday, like the Prophet Daniel, she would be able to say, "You've been weighed in the balances and found wanting."

As if guessing at what was on her mind, he said to her one day: "I think it's time for us to find some other kind of business, Léia. We're barely making ends meet as it is now. As you know well, I can't even afford to take you and the children to the seaside."

She looked at him carefully. "I think so too," she said with a note of suspicion in her voice.

Mayer laughed. "I'll show you what I'm capable of."

That night he went to Leib Kirschblum. "I'd like to make you a proposition, Leib . . ."

They stood talking until the small hours. When he got home, Léia was already asleep.

"We've just given birth to Maykir," he murmured, taking his shoes off.

Léia sat up in bed. "What have you been up to, Mayer? Not another of your crazy ideas to upset us, is it?"

"Relax, Léia," he replied. "This time I'm going to work for us. For you, for the children. You'll see. Just give me . . . four years. That's all I need. Four years."

1952

1952 WAS THE YEAR OF MAYKIR, THE REAL ESTATE
development company founded by Mayer Guinzburg and Leib
Kirschblum. The real estate business was booming in Porto Alegre; new buildings had mushroomed all over Bom Fim. Maykir
built buildings in great series. In the series called "Major Prophets" (the Isaiah Edifice, the Ezekiel Edifice, the Jeremiah Edifice, and so on,) the buildings had yellow granite façades and
eight apartments each. In the series called "Minor Prophets" (the
Zachariah Edifice, the Obadiah Edifice, and so on), the buildings also had yellow granite façades, but only six apartments each.
In the series "the Ten Commandments," the buildings had six
apartments each, but the façades were pink granite. The large
nameplate bearing the name "Maykir" could be seen everywhere
on Rua Felipe Camarão, on Rua Henrique Dias, on Rua Fernan-
Vieira, on Rua Augusto Pestana, on Rua Jacinto Gomes.

Maykir's headquarters were located in an old converted mansion
on Rua Fernandes Vieira. Its halls were always teeming with people: engineers, construction foremen, real estate agents, painters,
bricklayers, electricians, draftsmen, carpenters, contractors, work

ers specializing in terrazzo and parquet flooring. In Mayer's and Leib's offices, located upstairs, there were always crowds of sweaty, wide-eyed people talking in loud voices. The telephones never stopped ringing and couriers scurried about like mice.

Maykir. Maykir would build, incorporate, lease, sell. Maykir was a gigantic machine that creaked, crackled, and groaned as it ran—and yet it ran quite efficiently. Mayer Guinzburg's four-year plan had worked out well. He had thought out every single detail. "The secret lies in man himself!" he would say, and these words were quoted with respect and admiration throughout Bom Fim: in the furniture and the ready-to-wear stores, in the synagogues, at the Serafim, at the Israelite Social Circle.

Mayer Guinzburg negotiated the purchase of Marc Friedmann's old property in Beco do Salso. It was a much-talked-about transaction: it was rumored that Marc Friedmann at first had refused to sell; that Mayer Guinzburg, to pressure him, had threatened to divulge Marc's relationship with one of the company's employees—a pleasant young man with a dark complexion. Finally, however, Maykir succeeded in taking over the old hobby farm, and Mayer turned it into a club for his employees. There were spectacular things to be seen there, such as the grandiose flagpole made of concrete. Every Monday morning, the flag displaying the Maykir symbol—an *M* intertwined with a slide rule, a bricklayer's trowel, and a concrete mixer in silhouette—was raised on this flagpole. The honor of raising the flag was given to the employee that had stood out among his fellow workers in the previous week. During the ceremony, the Employees' Chorus intoned the Maykir Hymn:

> *"Maykir, Maykir, Maykir,*
> *With thee we shall rise!"*

On the property, Mayer Guinzburg built a swimming pool and a large pavilion suitable for parties and sports activities. Ev-

ery Thursday, Mayer went to the pavilion to give a speech on
the real estate market. The old house was kept in its original
condition. Mayer intended to turn it into a museum, the Maykir
Museum, where such things as the first tools used by the company's workers, old blueprints, and Mayer's own drawings would
be on display. He also sponsored the publication of *The Voice of
Maykir*, which came out every Tuesday; it was a magnificent
newsletter, profusely illustrated. Mayer himself wrote the editorial, in which he urged the bricklayers to lay more bricks, the
real estate agents to sell more real estate, and the typists to make
fewer mistakes. It was followed by a commentary on the current situation of the company. Then there was a report on the
amazing increase in sales—somewhat exaggerated, as Mayer was
the first the admit, but psychologically quite effective. The
newsletter also transcribed sections of *The Handbook of the Maykir
Employee* and provided its readers with news about the buildings
under construction: "The Daniel Edifice is now up to the third
floor! The construction of the Gemara Edifice will begin later
this week!" In addition, there was a gossip column: "It has been
rumored that a certain engineer is having an affair with a certain typist ..." The general consensus was that Mayer was a
real father to his employees. Under a pseudonym, he wrote a lonely
hearts column. And he also found time to devise crossword puzzles for the leisure section: "Document signed by both landlord
and tenant ... five letters." On Wednesdays he played volley-
ball with a group of employees, who vied with one another to
join his team.

Leib Kirschblum considered such things a waste of time and
money. "It's all part of the four-year plan," Mayer would explain.

1952. Mayer Guinzburg now lived in a spacious apartment on
Rua Ramiro Barcelos, located in a recently developed district.
He would get up early in the morning; while shaving, he would
whisper to himself the closing remarks of his speeches: "... the
engineers will design and construct, the construction foremen will

oversee, the workers will work, the buildings will rise, the real estate agents will sell!" Standing on the big marble sink, the little men watched him in silence. In her bathroom, Léia was also getting ready; although she didn't have to work anymore, she still had the habit of getting up early. The chauffeur would pick her up at eight o'clock; at eight-fifteen she was already downtown at work on one of her charity drives. In his bathroom, Jorge whistled as he shaved; he was enrolled in a pre-university course, and would be attending the School of Economics. Raquel's bathroom was unoccupied; she was still sound asleep, hugging her doll. Mayer Guinzburg worried about the girl, about her long silences, about her mania for reading until the small hours, about her spells of crying for which there was no apparent reason. Mayer Guinzburg studied himself in the mirror: He was now a well-dressed man, full of energy. Mayer Guinzburg, 1952.

1952. In the Soviet Union, Jewish doctors are accused of plotting against Stalin. In Czechoslovakia, Rudolf Slansky, who had been secretary-general of the Czech Communist party until 1950 and deputy prime minister until 1951, is put on trial for allegedly having engaged in "Trotskyite-Titoist-Sino activities, and for being in the pay of American imperialism ..." In December, 1952, Slansky and seven other Jewish defendants are found guilty and executed. 1952.

1952. Exuding energy, Mayer Guinzburg plunged himself into the task of erecting still more buildings. As soon as he finished shaving, he rushed to Rua Ferreira de Abreu, where, in an empty lot, many people—engineers, construction foremen, real estate agents, and even newsmen—were already waiting for him. As the Maykir flag rose on an improvised mast, Mayer announced, his voice quivering with emotion: "At this moment we initiate the construction of a new series of buildings—'the Kings of Israel'!"

The men applauded enthusiastically while the loudspeaker poured out the first few bars of the Maykir hymn:

"Maykir, Maykir, Maykir,
We're all smiles as we work for thee!"

1952.

1956

Nᴇᴡ ʏᴇᴀʀs ᴄᴀᴍᴇ ᴀɴᴅ ᴡᴇɴᴛ: 1953, 1954, 1955, and even 1956. At Maykir's, each new year was greeted with the popping sounds of champagne bottles being uncorked. New construction materials had been developed; more powerful cars were put at Mayer's disposal. In 1955 he didn't feel well; there was some kind of pain in his chest. He consulted Dr. Finkelstein, who advised him to slow down. He spent a weekend on the beach in Capão da Canoa and felt better; however, on Monday morning he had a headache when he arrived at the office. He asked Leib Kirschblum to look after the real estate agents, then went to his office and closed the door. He took an aspirin, leaned back in his comfortable swivel chair and decided he would sit there quietly until the headache was gone—even though there was plenty of work to be done. Right away, however, the intercom buzzed. The receptionist announced that Mr. José Goldman was there to see him. Mayer Guinzburg sighed. He hardly ever saw José Goldman these days; and he didn't really want to see much of him. They had been comrades once, it was true, but then their paths had diverged. Mayer Guinzburg had wanted to build a new society—and in a way he still did—but on his own plot of land and on his own initiative. Unlike José Goldman. It was rumored that he had connections; dangerous connections. Mayer was trying to guess the reason for this visit: José Goldman probably wanted to sell him books or raffle tickets, but Mayer was unwilling to have his name in heaven knows what kind of list or notebook. He was about to ask the receptionist to tell him he wasn't in—but José Goldman was already crossing the threshold.

"The receptionist said I could come in . . ."

How old we've grown, Mayer said to himself as he looked at the thin little man with white hair now standing in front of him. Controlling his irritation, Mayer asked him to sit down. They talked about trivial matters; and it was only when José Goldman tackled the subject of the world situation that Mayer noticed in his eyes that old glitter of thirty years before. Because at that moment José Goldman was transfigured: He was no longer addressing merely Mayer; he was now delivering a speech to a large crowd; the peroration went on and on, interrupted only, so it seemed, by the loud applause of the invisible audience.

"No," José Goldman was saying, "I don't believe in what is being said about Stalin. It's nothing but a defamation campaign engendered by the Social Democrats and the petite bourgeoisie . . ." (Applause.) "Yes," José Goldman went on, "it's obvious that the state of Israel is the spearhead of imperialism in the Middle East . . ." (Applause.) "Yes," he concluded, "I do believe we still have the right conditions to build a just society . . ."

Applause. Applause. Mayer asked him point-blank what he wanted. José Goldman stopped talking, and blushed.

"I'm sorry," said Mayer, somewhat embarrassed, "but I'm a very busy man."

"I know," said José Goldman. And then, with a little laugh: "Are you undergoing psychoanalysis?"

"Why?" asked Mayer, surprised.

"Because analysts don't beat around the bush. I went to see one, so I know ... Anyhow, let's get straight to the point. Time is money, isn't it, Mayer? I've never accepted it—I mean, this money power. People say I'm neurotic. My wife made me go to a psychiatrist. Not that I believe in such things; no, I don't. Pavlov is against all this nonsense. Pavlov carried out experiments ..."

Next, he was ranting on and on about something else. Mayer cut him short again. José Goldman sighed. Then he said that he was going through a difficult phase, that he couldn't bear life in a bourgeois society, that the decay—

"And what is it that you want?" asked Mayer, impatiently. "Is it money?"

José Goldman stared at him, offended.

"What do you take me for, Mayer? A schnorrer, a beggar? Well, let me tell you—"

"Is it a job, then?"

"Well, yes. But it isn't for me. I have a job, as you know, selling books. By the way, if you're interested in something—for your children, you know—I have some very good books—"

"Who's the job for?" Mayer realized that he was shouting. He could barely control himself. "Who is it for?"

"My daughter, Geórgia ... You know her, don't you? She and your daughter are friends ... You've met her, haven't you?"

Mayer couldn't remember if he had.

"She goes to college, she's in social sciences," José Goldman went on. "I think it's nonsense; instead of *studying* society, she should *change* society. That's what I keep telling her, but she won't listen to me. She doesn't show much respect for her father. Anyhow ... she has to pay for her tuition fees and I promised her I would try to get her a job."

Mayer turned the matter over in his mind for a while. In fact, he had been considering hiring a secretary: Leib Kirschblum would frown on it, but Mayer was convinced that a secretary would enhance his position as director. He told José Goldman to send the young woman to his office that same afternoon.

She came.

Geórgia. She had been named after Stalin's birthplace. She was somewhat older than Raquel: freckles, big blue eyes, short hair, and a set smile on her face. Mayer had already obtained information on her. "People talk about her," Leib warned.

"I know how to pick people for my team!" replied Mayer. Leib fell silent. He disapproved of these modern expressions. Team, indeed! Shamelessness, that's what it amounted to.

After interviewing Geórgia, Mayer decided to hire her. The real estate agents were delighted, and so was everybody else— the engineers, the draftsmen, the construction foremen.

On the following Sunday, Mayer saw Geórgia at the Maykir Club. She was lying by the swimming pool, stretched out on a towel. Mayer gazed at her beautiful legs, at her belly heaving gently in the sun, at her closed eyes. On Monday, as he shaved, Mayer inspected his own face. I'm a vigorous man. Macho! he said to himself. He knows what is going to happen: One of these days there will be some extra work to be finished; he'll ask Geórgia to stay on at the office; he'll be dictating letters to her; he'll be pacing the office up and down; suddenly, he'll stop behind her, and bend over her smooth neck to kiss it . . .

They'll make love on the big leather couch; the phone will ring, but they won't answer it; her stomach will rumble and they'll break into laughter. Then, still lying on the couch, she'll smoke, and Mayer will feel tired but satiated. Out of the corner of his eye he'll see the little men standing on the big jacaranda table. They'll be waiting for Mayer to say something, at least one word. "We're about to begin . . ." Mayer will mumble the words and stop abruptly. The little men will applaud discreetly.

1956 was a very busy year at Maykir's, so busy that Mayer

Guinzburg often had to ask Geórgia to stay on at the office. When Leib Kirschblum walked down Rua Fernandes Vieira in the evening and saw the lights on in Mayer's office he would shake his head. Soon the real estate agents began whispering, and so did everybody else—the engineers, the construction foremen, the bricklayers, the carpenters. Somebody had hoisted a flag on the club's flagpole: It depicted Geórgia typing as she sat on Mayer's lap. And there were cartoons, too, collected in an album titled "Captain Birobidjan's Adventures," which circulated clandestinely among the Maykir employees. This album, still extant, was beautifully bound. The *first drawing* depicts Mayer Guinzburg at the moment of hiring Geórgia. "Take off your clothes," reads the caption. In the *second drawing*, Mayer points to a chart illustrating the rising profits of his enterprise; as a pointer, he uses his own gigantic penis, while an entranced Geórgia looks on. The caption reads, "How to rise in life without any effort." The *third drawing* depicts Geórgia holding several miniature buildings in her arms; fully dressed, she is sitting on Mayer's chest, and he groans under her weight. The caption reads: "Maykir's security lies on solid foundations."

The typists kept whispering; the tenants kept whispering. Mayer Guinzburg became the favorite conversation topic of the women shopping up and down Rua Felipe Camarão, or on their way to the market. "He's killing his wife and children!" they would say, outraged. They demanded that their husbands do something about this situation. Leib Kirschblum's wife urged him to talk to his partner. He plucked up enough courage to see Mayer in his office: "It's none of my business. However ..." At that moment Geórgia walked in. Leib Kirschblum fell silent and never brought up the subject again.

Geórgia was growing more and more insolent. She would address Mayer informally in front of everybody; when he reprimanded her, she would retort with sarcasm: "All right, Captain Birobidjan!" Mayer could barely control his anger. It now seemed to him that the leather couch had grown narrower and that there was hardly any room for the two of them. "Get up," he'd mutter, panting. "Why don't *you* get up," she'd snap back. "Who's the man around here? Who's the gentleman?" Mayer remained silent. Then one night Geórgia said, lighting a cigarette: "I was talking to Raquel at the club yesterday. I don't think she'll object ..."

"Object to what?" asked Mayer, alarmed.

"To your getting a separation. I've been thinking about it and it seems to me that your wife—"

Mayer cut her short. "Are you now meddling with my family?" he yelled. He got to his feet and was standing on the couch. "You? A venomous spider, a perfidious hen? How dare you, a mere employee, a slave! Get out of here!"

Geórgia left in tears. Mayer sighed; then he let himself collapse on the couch, where he remained for a long time. Finally, he got up and went home.

On the following day, Geórgia asked for his forgiveness and they made up; however, Mayer knew that their reconciliation wouldn't last long. He was a vigorous man. Geórgia had made the mistake of trying to hold sway over him and she was going to pay for this mistake.

1956. The end of the year was quite stressful. Maykir's financial commitments had been growing larger; the newspapers were full of reports about an imminent war between Israel and its neighbors. Mayer had been avoiding Geórgia. At work he treated her coldly; she was no longer asked to stay on at the office, notwithstanding a backlog of work. Finally, however, Geórgia succeeded in making a rendezvous with Mayer. They met in a rooming house at Praia de Belas on October 30, 1956. It was in the afternoon. Mayer Guinzburg arrived quite late and began shouting as soon as he walked into the room: "Why are you sitting by the window? So that the entire world can see you?"

Geórgia tried to hug him. He pushed her away. He was upset, he told her, about Israel's attack on Egypt.

"Last night, and without any warning whatsoever, Israeli troops
invaded the Sinai."

"But Mayer, there have been all those provocations," she said,
surprised. "On September 23, the Jordanians attacked the members of an archaeological group that was inspecting the diggings
at Ramat Rachel. All of a sudden, from an Arab Legion post,
came a burst of machine-gun fire, killing eight people and wound-
ing eighteen."*

"But the Jordanians said that only one person was responsible
for the attack, a soldier of the Arab Legion who suddenly went
crazy and ..."

"And yet, on that very same day, the Jordanians shot two other
Israelis—a farmer in Maoz Chaim and a woman on the out-
skirts of Jerusalem. And on the border with Egypt, five travelers
were killed on the Sodom-Beersheba road. And infiltrators invaded an orange grove near Even Hehuduh; they killed two workers and cut off their ears."

"And on the following day," Mayer shouted, "Israeli forces destroyed a Jordanian police station at Kalkilya. It's outrageous!
Right there on Jordanian territory!"

He was shaking with rage. Geórgia turned pale.

"I'd like to remind you, Mayer, that during these last two weeks
the Egyptians have recommenced their attacks in the south.
Fedayee units have mined Israeli territory and three Israeli sol-
diers were killed when a mine went off as their vehicle drove
through the area."

Mayer fell silent. He stood gazing at her face, at her big eyes,

---

*"These words, as well as all the others in this dialogue, are direct quotes from statements
made by Ben Gurion, Bulganin, and other heads of state involved in the events that took place at
that time," said Mayer's niece, the history professor. "But no mention is ever made of the sources
of information," added the librarian. "That's what I mean when I say there aren't bibliographical
references."

at her lips, which were trembling a little. He felt like taking her in his arms and starting all over again. But he fought off the feeling.

"There's no room in history for this kind of sentimentality. In addition, Israel mobilized its reserves and deployed as many of its troops as possible near its borders."

She wiped her tears and took a deep breath. She made an effort to look him in the face, without showing any signs of weakness: "That was merely a reaction. What else could they do to face the unified commandos of Egypt, Syria, and Jordan, not to mention the Egyptian raids on Israel? The Israeli government would be showing disregard for their fundamental responsibilities if they didn't take all possible measures to thwart the Arab rulers' stated decision to suppress Israel by force . . ."

Mayer jumped to his feet. "It wasn't like that at all! The Israeli government set up a treacherous attack on its neighbors, obeying foreign orders. Israel was in collusion with England and France—two imperialistic superpowers—to invade Egypt. Israel is a perfidious nation—just as perfidious as you are. What you're after is my money . . ."

"Stop it!" She was unable to control herself any longer. She burst into tears. Then she gradually calmed down.

Seated by the window, Mayer watched her in silence. She walked up to him.

"Why are you so horrible to me, Mayer? Haven't I given you moments of pleasure? I don't—"

"They're mine," Mayer said, cutting her short. "They belong to me. All my memories. You have nothing to do with them."

"All right, Mayer," she murmured. "I don't want to take anything away from you. All I want is . . ." She knelt down by his side. "Why don't we go away, Mayer? Let's go somewhere far away from here, and build our lives there. It could be like New Birobidjan—remember what you used to tell me?"

102

"You made fun of me!" said Mayer gloomily.

"I didn't understand you then, Mayer. Now I know what it was that you were trying to tell me—that we must abjure the barrenness of this life. This barren life. Let's go, Mayer! To New Birobidjan! Hmm? I'll be your comrade—Comrade Geórgia. Together we'll rebuild everything. The flagpole, the Palace of Culture; together we'll choose the site of the future power plant ... And you'll be the chairman of the Political Committee, the president of the People's University, the generalissimo, everything you've always wanted to be. And I'll obey you. You'll give speeches, and I'll listen to them and then ask interesting questions. And I'll read *The Voice of New Birobidjan*—the editorial will stimulate my mind; the commentary will warn me; the news items will inform me; the crossword puzzle will entertain me; the jokes will make me laugh ... I'll till the land, I'll increase productivity ..."

"Cut out the litany, will you?" said Mayer, bored. "You sound like a rabbi."

Yes, he was thinking, suppose I go away with her. Then one day she'll walk out on me, and I'll be left alone, and will sleep in the mansion, with the skulls of Comrade Pig and Comrade Goat. Yes, one day she'll take off, just like Comrade Hen. And he ... he would wander about, stumbling on the charred remains of the Palace of Culture. He would sit down on a rock, mulling over what life is and might have been. And would he be able to take it? The loneliness—would he be able to take it? No. He would end up talking to himself. From eight to nine o'clock he would deliver a panegyric on Stalin, the father of socialism, humanity's beacon. From nine to ten o'clock he would deliver a diatribe against Stalin—an assassin, an insensitive, cold-blooded tyrant. The little men, befuddled, wouldn't know when to applaud. Madness. Sheer madness.

"It's a waste of time, Geórgia. You'd better go now."

She got to her feet. She was smiling.

"A waste of time? I can afford to waste time. I'm young. There'll be plenty of other men in the years ahead."

"A know-it-all, aren't you?" said Mayer with irritation. "Well, let me tell you something. There's more life experience accumulated under the nail of my little finger than there is in your whole body."

"Not an ugly body, is it, Mayer?" she sneered. "It's still going to give pleasure to lots of people ..."

"Is it?" Mayer drew nearer. "Is it really? How can you be sure you won't be run over at the intersection over there? How can you be sure that some sex maniac isn't going to strangle you tonight?"

He put his fingers around her throat. Geórgia managed to extricate herself.

"Don't be such an idiot, you old coot. You know very well I'm not about to die. You're the one who already has one foot in the grave. The way you lie huffing and puffing, limp like an old rag, after you ... And that pain in your chest. You've been having an awful lot of chest pains, haven't you?"

"Okay, so I'm going to die. Thank God I ..."

"God?!" She burst into laughter. "Since when have you believed in God?"

Mayer didn't know; for some time now. The belief had gradually crept up on him. Now he often read the Torah, the Mishnah, the Gemara. He intoned his prayers the way his father used to: swaying his body back and forth.

"Who knows, maybe death is the ultimate wager. I've had a good life, in my own way, of course. But what about you? You haven't even fulfilled the dream of every young Jewish girl: to get married. And now you'll be drifting all alone. Will you find another Mayer Guinzburg? Another old idiot like me?"

"Good-bye, Captain," she said, and left.

Mayer Guinzburg remained seated for a while. Then he picked up his hat and left too.

He drove slowly to Redenção Park. He got out of the car and began to walk along the graveled paths. He walked past the aviary, past the monkeys' cage. He thought he would rent a small boat and row for a while but the ticket office was already closed.

Night was falling. Mayer had dinner in a small *churrascaria*, a restaurant that served barbecued meat, Brazilian style. He ate a large meal: filet of beef, chicken, tenderloin, fish, polenta, potato salad, wine. When he wanted to get into his car he couldn't because he had lost the car keys. He walked home slowly, belching at times.

As he approached his apartment house, a figure stepped out of the shadows and advanced toward him. It was José Goldman.

"Captain! Captain Birobidjan, you filthy bastard!"

Mayer Guinzburg stopped. The other man grabbed him by the coat.

"What have you done to my daughter, you pig?"

"Wait a moment, Goldman—" Mayer began.

"The state she's in. Drunk! A girl who's never tasted a drop of alcohol! You made this wretched girl drunk, you cur!"

"Me, Goldman?" Mayer took a step back.

"Yes, you! Your name, that's all she keeps repeating. And she's been phoning you at home."

"But, Goldman—"

"The same old tactics, isn't it? To hoodwink, to delude, to corrupt in order to conquer!"

"But we were just having a conversation ... We were talking about Israel ..."

"A damn lie!" José Goldman's rage was growing. "Israel! I'll show you Israel! The promised land, right? The Kibbutzim, Ben Gurion, right? I'll show you, you scoundrel!"

He let go of Mayer's coat and pulled out a knife.

"Goldman!" Mayer shouted, frightened. "That's not something a Jew would do—pull a knife on a friend."

"Oh, yeah! I'll show you!"

105

Mayer broke into a run. José Goldman chased him for a while, then he tripped and fell. Mayer was out of breath when he reached his apartment building. He tried to insert the key into the keyhole but couldn't: His hands were shaking violently. He thought he could hear José Goldman's footsteps behind him.

"Help me, oh God, help me, just this once. I'll never again ... just this once ..." Finally, he succeeded in unlocking the front door. He burst into his apartment and flopped onto the big couch, where he lay panting. Gradually he regained his composure and was then overcome by a sensation of well-being—of euphoria, even. "That was a pretty narrow escape! But I'm free now! I've escaped from both father and daughter." Suddenly an amusing idea crossed his mind: He would go to the kitchen, raid the fridge, set food galore on the table, and glut himself. He sprang to his feet. "Nothing like food to lift one's spirits!"

The light was on in the kitchen. Mayer opened the door to find Léia sitting there. The table was empty.

"Somebody's been phoning you," she said. "Several times, leaving messages."

"Léia—" he began. His wife got up and advanced upon him.

In the *kitchen*, she hurled the *food processor* and the *blender* at him; in the *living room*, she hit him with the *TV antenna*; in the *bathroom*, she tried to drown him in the *marble sink*; in the *hall*, she hurled *pictures, statuettes*, and even an old *samovar* at him. Their son was trying to separate them; Raquel stood crying in a corner. Léia removed her wedding ring and was trying to shove it into her husband's mouth.

"Eat it, you shameless creature! Eat it, you scoundrel!"

☆☆☆☆☆☆☆☆☆☆☆☆☆☆☆☆☆☆☆☆☆☆☆☆☆☆☆☆☆☆☆☆☆☆☆☆☆

1957

SEPARATED FROM HIS WIFE, MAYER GUINZBURG WENT to live in a hotel for a while. He wanted to rent an apartment, but Maykir didn't have any available at the moment. Finally, he had an idea: He requested that an apartment be prepared for him in the King David Edifice, which was still under construction, and then moved in. Leib Kirschblum didn't dare to oppose him. "He'll be in a better position to supervise the construction work," he explained to his friends in an apologetic tone. Leib Kirschblum also took upon himself the task of appeasing José Goldman, who claimed to have in his possession some political documents signed by Mayer Guinzburg (an issue of *The Voice of New Birobidjan*). "I could get him into a lot of hot water," José Goldman kept saying. "You? But you have much more to lose than he does," Leib Kirschblum reasoned. "I don't care," replied José Goldman. "I want to see him behind bars, even if it means we'll be there together." At long last Leib Kirschblum succeeded in dissuading him.

Mayer furnished his apartment sparingly. At first, he hardly spent any time there; he left quite early in the morning, had breakfast at the Serafim, and then went to his office. He had lunch and dinner in a *churrascaria*. He would go home only at night; he hated walking down the deserted halls of the building.

The King David was huge. The halls were still cluttered with construction materials, the walls hadn't been stuccoed yet, and some of the scaffolding was still in place. Mayer would enter his apartment, take a tranquilizer, and lie down. He would wake up in the middle of the night to the sound of strange noises. The wind would blow through the openings; the entire structure would creak, crackle, and groan. Toward dawn he would drift off to an uneasy sleep, soon interrupted by the dull booming sounds of the explosions in the construction site next to the King David; there the King Solomon, another building in the Kings of Israel series, would be erected. The explosions shattered most of the windowpanes that had been recently installed in Mayer's apartment, but he could'nt have cared less.

He was getting used to his new life, and beginning to enjoy his place. Unawares, he is already making plans for changes in the building: The playground will give way to corn and bean patches; the top floor will house the Palace of Culture. In front of the building, there will be a gigantic flagpole, on which he'll raise the flag of New Birobidjan. He has already found comrades to carry out his enterprise: a mouse, who lives in one of the bins storing construction materials; a spider with thin, delicate legs, who lives in her own cobweb on the fourth floor; and an odd insect, a cross between a fly and a cockroach, who sometimes flutters about the light bulb. Mayer doesn't really like him; he doesn't know why, but he dislikes him. In spite of his self-criticism, Mayer continues to dislike him.

To Mayer, the King David had acquired a new dimension. In the morning he no longer felt the urge to rush to work; on the contrary, now he preferred to cook his own meals in the apartment, where sometimes he would spend the whole day. Leib Kirschblum began to worry; business wasn't doing well, and he needed his partner's full attention. He would go to the King David every day to beg of Mayer that he go to the office. Only reluctantly would Mayer acquiesce.

And then Mayer would shut himself up in his office for hours on end, speaking to no one. One afternoon he got a phone call: a frightened voice asked him to hurry to the King David without delay. The building had just collapsed.

Mayer Guinzburg drove there. From behind sunglasses, and without getting out of the car, he looked at the rubble of brick and twisted steel. An article of bedding caught on a large iron bar reminded him of a flag.

As soon as he returned to his office, he burst into Leib Kirschblum's room: "You idiot, you fool!"

"What's the matter," groaned Leib Kirschblum, startled.

"What's the matter, you may well ask. Go and see the King David. It has collapsed. I could have been killed!" He was pacing back and forth. "I had anticipated this would happen. It was because of the King Solomon! The explosions rocked the King David. I knew this was bound to happen. The broken window-panes, the cracks in the walls ..."

"But why in the world didn't you warn us?" groaned his partner. "You were the only person that entered the King David. You wouldn't even allow the workers in there ..."

"You know very well," Mayer shouted, "that I don't meddle in your projects!"

"*My* projects?!" It was Leib Kirschblum's turn to shout. "But the King David and the King Solomon were *your* projects! You said you would supervise the construction work personally because the engineer—who's a nephew of yours, by the way—was incompetent!"

"That's ... that's a damn lie," spluttered Mayer with disbelief. Leib Kirschblum pulled a drawer open.

"Here, look! Purchase requests, work authorization slips, payrolls—with your signature on every single one of them!"

He hurled the documents at Mayer, who beat a retreat. Leib Kirschblum chased him throughout Maykir's headquarters. In the *draftsmen's room*, he hit him with a *T-square* and a *ruler*; in the *accounting department*, he hurled a *calculating machine* at him; in the reception room, he tried to strangle him with the *telephone cord*. At long last people succeeded in separating them.

A few months later Maykir went bankrupt.

1958, 1959, 1960 . . . 1966

MAYER GUINZBURG RENTED A SMALL APARTMENT
and went job hunting. He thought that it wouldn't be difficult
for an entrepreneur like himself to find a job. However, the op-
posite was the case. Nobody wanted to hire him. "Sorry, Mayer ..."
Some of them would say. Others had sharp words for him.
"You've been bad-mouthing Israel," a Zionist told him. "Me?
But I've even named my buildings after kings and prophets ..."
"Ah, yes. Kings and prophets," the other replied. "Ancient history. Nowadays things are different, aren't they? Nowadays Israel is no good, right? You think I don't know that you vilified
Israel to that floozy, José Goldman's daughter?" Others wouldn't
mince words: "You're nuts, Mayer. You belong in a loony bin!"

At last he reconciled himself to taking money from his son,
now an economist, who also owned a supermarket. At first
Mayer had refused to accept what he regarded as charity but
changed his mind when the unpaid bills began to pile up. He
was always entering into arguments with Jorge. The young man
admired the Americans.

"Great people! Enterprising, businesslike!"

"They want to take over the world," Mayer muttered.

"And what's wrong with that?" Jorge laughed.

"What's wrong?" Mayer was furious. "And are you going to let yourself be taken over?"

"What's wrong with that?"

He would leave the envelope with the money and depart. "What's wrong, indeed?" Mayer wondered. "It really doesn't make any difference to me, after all. Americans? Who are they? Russians, Englishmen . . . I don't think I've ever met an Englishman—or have I?"

From the top of the chest of drawers the little men watched him in silence.

One day Mayer examined them closely.

They were very short: not more than ten centimeters tall. Although he had always seen them as "little men," he noticed that there were also little women among them. The little people were far fewer than he had at first thought: a dozen, at the most. One of them, who had a big mustache, looked like Stalin. Some of them were old. He could detect tiny wrinkles on their tiny faces; their bald heads shone in the weak lamplight. Some of the tiny hands shook slightly and sometimes he could hear a dry cough. They stood looking at him in a state of silent expectancy. Mayer Guinzburg sighed and went out.

He used to go for walks all over the city. He would go to Bom Fim, which had changed substantially. The buildings that he had built, the Kings and the Prophets were now dwarfed by modern high rises with intercom systems replacing the doormen. Downtown, he would watch the elderly men sitting in Praça da Alfândega—some talked to each other; others just sat silently. I'm about ready for old age; he would say to himself. All I need is a scarf, a pipe, heavily lined slippers, an enlarged prostate . . . Depressed, he would return to his apartment. Unsuccessfully, he tried to think of cultivated fields, of the Palace of Culture, of masts and flags; but the spiders that appeared in his

apartment were just spiders, and the insects, just insects. They
would drop into the soup that Mayer had laboriously prepared,
filling him with loathing and displeasure. The first time when
one of the fly buttons in his pants came off, he took the trouble
of sewing on another; when it happened again, he tried to re-
place it but his hands shook so badly that he gave up the idea. I
should get some of those pants with zippers, he said to himself. But would he be able to unzip them? With his fingers
trembling like that? What if the zipper got stuck at the very
moment when he had the urge to urinate? Three more buttons
came off his fly; he couldn't care less.

Jorge chided him: "Just look at the state of your clothes." He
brought Mayer a new pair of pants with zippers, and Mayer
gave them to a beggar who often asked for alms.

"How's Léia these days? And Raquel?" he would ask his son.
Léia was fine; she never came to see him. Raquel had come
once, and burst into tears. Mayer asked Jorge not to bring her
anymore.

Early in 1966, Mayer had a dream. He is walking along a deserted street. Night has fallen and Mayer begins to walk fast
because he knows that José Goldman is lurking somewhere. All
of a sudden, a black car pulls over. Two men alight, push him
inside the car, and then they drive off. Terror-stricken, Mayer
Guinzburg notices that his captors are wearing black masks; a
moment later, they put a hood over his face and he can't see anything. "Drive along Rua Protásio Alves," one of them says to
the driver. Ah, Mayer thinks, so we must be heading for Petrópolis.
Or could it be Três Figueiras? Or maybe Beco do Salso? He
tries to strike up a conversation; he asks questions, to which he
gets no replies.

The car is brought to a standstill. Mayer is forced to get out.
For a while he walks along a trail amid trees and shrubs. At
one moment he pretends to have tripped over something and he
picks up an object that is lying on the ground, hoping that later

it will help him identify the area. They push him into a house, make him sit on the floor, and at last, remove his hood. Even in the dark he is able to recognize the place: It's the house on the hobby farm formerly owned by Marc Friedmann.

"Mayer! Mayer Guinzburg!" shouts a voice in the dark. "We're holding you for ransom. We need money. We're beginning to build a new society."

Mayer's terror vanishes to be replaced by intense excitement. They want to build a new society! So, they must be friends! They haven't recognized him, but they must be friends.

"I'm behind you all the way!" he shouts. "Like you, I'm building a new society too!"

They laugh at him. At this exploiter. At this dirty capitalist. "A new society? Some society! A corporation, that's what your new society is!" Disconcerted, Mayer Guinzburg falls silent.

"We're holding you for ransom," says the same voice again. "We're demanding one hundred thousand."

"One hundred thousand cruzeiros?"

"Dollars."

Strong currency, Mayer says to himself. They know what they want. The negotiations will be tough, though.

"You won't get all this money," he states.

"No? And what about your family?"

"My family!" Mayer laughs. "They don't give a damn about me. My pants are missing buttons and nobody will sew new buttons on."

"What about Leib Kirschblum?"

"He ... ?" Mayer's mind goes blank; he seems unable to recall things very clearly. Leib Kirschblum ... Are they still business partners? Haven't the buildings collapsed? He decides to make a deal with his captors. "Leib Kirschblum isn't going to fork over any money. He ... he broke with me. Let's not waste any time. I'll give you a check ..."

114

"A check?" said one of the captors, whose face Mayer couldn't see very well. "And where can we get it cashed?"

He laughs. "You'll get it cashed all right," Mayer states. "I guarantee. Deep down you must know that I'm behind you all the way."

Mayer hears them whispering together. Finally, one of his captors addresses him.

"How much?"

"Twenty thousand," says Mayer.

"Dollars?"

"Cruzeiros. I've been through difficult times."

"Thirty thousand."

"No way . . ."

They settle for twenty-five thousand. He makes out a check and gets to his feet.

"You're staying here," says a voice, "until we cash the check."

"But it's nighttime," says Mayer. "It's dark. The banks are closed."

"The check will bounce, is that it?"

"What do you mean?" Mayer mumbles. "What kind of logic is this, if it's dark then the check must be worthless?"

Hands grab him roughly and search through his pockets.

"Look at this!"

A lantern sheds light on the object that Mayer picked up earlier on the trail. He sees a bird's skull. Mayer Guinzburg's eyes brim with tears; now he realizes what happened to Comrade Hen. "I've been unfair," he murmurs.

"We know," the voice shouts. "That you've been unfair, we know."

Suddenly they find themselves on the beach in Capão da Canoa. Some men whom he has never seen before pick him up brutally and hurl him into the sea.

And in this sea he is now afloat, half-drowned, while distant sounds reach his ears: The explosions in the King Solomon Edifice?

The knocking on the door wakes him from his sleep. It's Jorge. Mayer Guinzburg is surprised at this early morning visit. They talk for a while. Suddenly Jorge looks around him and says: "You're far from being comfortable here, Father."

"What?" Mayer is amazed. "What makes you say so?"

"Look at the dirt . . . Insects all over . . . And look at the state of your clothes—all torn. This apartment is not suitable. I have something better for you."

He starts talking about a boarding house for single people. Owned by a really nice lady, who is also an excellent cook. Located in beautiful, pleasant surroundings.

"Guess where?" says Jorge, with a smile. "In Beco do Salso. In the old house where the Maykir Club used to be. Leib Kirschblum sold it to this lady and she had it renovated . . ."

The words reach Mayer Guinzburg as if coming from a very long distance. It's as if I were at the bottom of the sea, he says to himself. Jorge keeps on talking and Mayer nods his agreement.

When she heard that someone was planning to write a book about Mayer Guinzburg, his niece, the sociologist, said: "I think that the greatest emphasis should be placed on the sociological aspects. Thus, social mobility and hidden poverty can be better analyzed."

1967–1969

Aᴼᴼ ᴀᴄQᴜɪʀɪɴɢ ᴛʜᴇ ꜰᴏʀᴍᴇʀ Mᴀʏᴋɪʀ Cʟᴜʙ, Dona Sofia (who happened to be a cousin of Leib Kirschblum's), had several things changed there. The old pavilion was dismantled and then sold; the house itself was converted into a boarding house; rooms were partitioned off to create several new bedrooms. Some of the old things were kept: The flagpole became a lamppost, and the old couch—refurbished with brown plastic—was placed in the living room.

There the boarders would congregate: Octávio Rodrigues, seventy-eight years old, a former grain dealer, nicknamed "the Portuguese"; an Egyptian Jew called David Benveniste, eighty-one; and a lady from Dom Pedrito, called Ana Souza. Not too many yet, Dona Sofia granted Jorge, but once more people found out about the boarding house, she told him, new boarders would come. However, the fact was that after Ana, the last of the three boarders to have moved in, there had been no other newcomers until a year and a half later, when Mayer Guinzburg arrived.

Dona Sofia showed him to his room, which was simply furnished with a bed, two chairs, and chest of drawers.

"There's only one bathroom," she explained, "so, everybody's cooperation is needed ... You understand, don't you?"

"I understand," murmured Mayer.

"They're all very refined people," Dona Sofia went on. "Octávio is very charming, a good conversationalist. David Benveniste used to be quite well-off there in Egypt ... where he was a very busy merchant. Then he lost everything. He emigrated to Brazil and after his wife's death, lived with his daughter until she got married. Their apartment was very small, so ..." She leaned toward Mayer. "He's not all there, don't pay attention to what he says ... Sometimes he attacks the Jews, hurls insults at them ... It's all very foolish, because he is a Jew too."

"I know," said Mayer.

Sofia Kirschblum. Born in Russia in 1908; never married. At eighteen years of age her weight was forty-six kilograms; at sixty, her weight was ninety. A strong, solidly built woman, she took pride in her enterprising abilities. Sofia Kirschblum.

On the first two days following his arrival, Mayer didn't leave his room. He claimed he wasn't feeling well, "due to the change of environment." Dona Sofia was very solicitous and she herself carried his meals to his room.

On the third day, having a distended belly, Mayer has the urge to go to the bathroom.

As he opens the door, he notices it hasn't got a latch; then he remembers the landlady's clearly stated warning: There's only one bathroom, which should not be monopolized. Mayer Guinzburg sits down on the toilet. Aware of the time limit, he strains at stool. He is in a sweat and even lets out a moan. Before he can produce anything, someone is already trying to push the door open.

"It's occupied," Mayer warns in a choked voice.

However, whoever is behind the door doesn't hear—or doesn't want to hear; whoever is behind the door believes—or wants to believe—that the door is stuck and the person keeps trying to

push it open. Mayer Guinzburg puts up resistance. "*No pasarán!*"
He succeeds in holding the door shut. His opponent gives up. A
few minutes later, a new onslaught. Could it be the same person again? Or is it someone else? It's irrelevant. "It's occupied,
it's occupied," Mayer keeps repeating; he looks around him,
searching for something that could be used as a makeshift latch.
He doesn't see anything suitable. His body is the barricade; but
seated, and having to lean forward like this, he's not in the best
position to hold the door shut. He substitutes one of his hands
with one of his feet. But the foot proves to be less strong than
the hand and he anxiously watches his shoe retreat at each blow
on the door. At this moment he begins to defecate. At long last!
He has one single wish now: That his foot not give in before
his bowels finish doing their business. They've finally done their
business, or rather, it just seems that they have, for Mayer feels
there is still more, and that he shouldn't keep things inside him.
The door, however, is already ajar! Mayer makes one last effort; he groans, turns purple, and behold! there goes the last frag-
ment. Just then the door begins to open wide. Oh God, let it
not be a woman! It isn't. It's David Benveniste, his ratlike face
already inside the bathroom. "Ah, it's the Russian Jew . . . These
Jews are always taking everything over!" Mayer's face breaks into
the sickly smile of the innocent caught red-handed. He tries to
get up. He can't: He's sitting awkwardly, far back, his buttocks
sagging down into the toilet. Benveniste has to pull him up.
Mayer Guinzburg is now on his feet, apologizing and expressing
his thanks. He feels relieved but his gratification is short-lived.
"It's disgraceful. At my age, to have to fight to use the bathroom, and to think that I've once owned this place . . ."

He goes to the living room, sits down on the couch, and looks
at his watch. Still another two hours before lunch. "It's disgraceful, I can't even eat when I feel like it . . ." Half an hour
later he gets up. He has decided to go to the bathroom. "I feel
like going again, and why not? Maybe I have diarrhea. Well, and

119

even if I don't, who's going to prevent me from sitting on the toilet rather than on the couch?" He walks down the hall and begins to push the bathroom door open.

"It's occupied!" says a feeble voice in a beseeching tone. It's David Benveniste.

Mayer Guinzburg pretends he hasn't heard; he keeps on pushing. The door yields, and he realizes that the enemy is not strong and that the citadel will fall. But then he hesitates. The bathroom is common territory; Mayer Guinzburg, the man who has fought for a better world, is not the person who will use force to oppress others. He lets go of the doorknob, and stands in the hall, his arms hanging down at his sides. Then the door opens; David Benveniste is still buttoning up his fly; a broad grin spreads over his jowls.

"Ah, here's my fellow countryman! Go in, go in. Stay there for as long as you want. We Jews have to be kind to each other."

Benveniste walks down the hall, mumbling to himself: "I'll have to take a purgative; nothing like a purgative to cleanse the body." Mayer enters the bathroom but soon leaves again. He goes back to the sitting room, where he finds the Egyptian seated on the couch. Mayer Guinzburg remains standing, looking at his watch; one hour and a half before lunch, one hour, fifteen minutes ... And now, lunchtime! Everybody sits down at the table.

"We're having some very good soup today," announces Dona Sofia as she brings a tureen to the table.

Ana Souza says she doesn't like soup. "This one is really good, quite nourishing," declares Dona Sofia, ladling out some soup.

"Eat."

Whimpering, Ana picks up her spoon.

After lunch Mayer returns to his room. He keeps pacing back and forth. From the top of the chest of drawers, the little men watch in silence. Their number has decreased: There are no more than six of them now.

Feeling tired, Mayer lies down and falls asleep. He has a dream: He is walking down a long hall, at the end of which is the bathroom. He opens the door and finds David Benveniste sitting there, reading a magazine.

"Magazines aren't allowed in the bathroom," Mayer protests.

"Shut up, Captain Birobidjan, and listen to this!" says Benveniste, who then proceeds to read aloud: " 'Whoever thinks that the Quixotes are an extinct race, is dead wrong, as Raquel Guinzburg (single, twenty-seven-years old, born in Rio Grande do Sul) and Colony Silva (separated, sixty-two-years old, also a native of this state) have proved. Raquel, the daughter of a former real estate entrepreneur, was living common-law with Colomy ...' "

"That's a damn lie! Not with that old man, of all people!" Mayer Guinzburg is outraged.

Ruthlessly, Benveniste continues to read.

" 'Raquel Guinzburg and Colomy used to read books by Rosa Luxemburg,' it says right here in this article. 'Inspired by her books, the two of them highjacked a Gloster Meteor airplane and then threatened to bomb downtown Porto Alegre if their demands for acquiring Beco do Salso were not met ...' "

"That's a lie! A lie!" Mayer shouts. "That man used to be an Integralista, a right-winger!"

" 'The authorities agreed to their demands,' " the Egyptian goes on. " 'When the airplane was about to land at the airport, workers began to roll oil drums all over the tarmac. The plane crashed against one of them and caught fire. Colomy died in the crash. Raquel committed suicide, shooting herself before ...' "

"That's a lie! A lie!"

Mayer wakes up. It's coffee time. He walks down the hall, heading for the dining room. He walks past the bathroom: The door is closed; he pushes it violently. There sits David Benveniste but without a magazine in his hands.

121

"What do you think you're doing, you Jew, barging in like this? Close the door!"

After finishing their coffee, Mayer Guinzburg and Octávio Rodrigues sit down on the couch to talk for a while.

"I've heard about a pirate called the Portuguese," Mayer says.

He quotes passages from Antônio Barata's book: "Audacity, fierceness, swaggering were some of the Portuguese's qualities. Once, off Cape Corrientes in Cuba, along with a handful of ragged men and practically weaponless, he attacked a ship armed with twenty guns. After seizing the ship, he changed into a gala uniform to impress the beautiful women passengers that he had captured. Later, however, when attempting to attack three other ships, he was defeated, held captive, and taken to Campeche, to be hanged. However, he succeeded in killing his jailer and in escaping from the ship where he was held prisoner. He had to reach the seashore. 'He wasn't a strong swimmer,' Antônio Barata writes, 'but he was brave enough to risk his life in order to find freedom.' He drained the wine out of two large jugs, tied them to his body as makeshift buoys, then climbed down the side of the ship. It was nighttime, and his escape went undetected. 'The Portuguese was afloat, motionless, half-drowned, while the large jugs tinkled as they carried him slowly across the waters,' writes Antônio Barata. Finally, he reached the shore, and after traveling a hundred forty miles on foot, he arrived at a pirates' settlement and there he was given a boat. Then he sailed back to Campeche, where he arrived at nightfall: '. . . the fading twilight outlined the gallows, from which hung the bodies of the Portuguese's former comrades. The hanged men, clustered in groups of two and three, were swaying in the evening breeze.' Using this gruesome scene to prod him into action, the Portuguese led his men in the attack against the enemy and succeeded in recapturing his former ship. This remarkable feat earned him everybody's admiration; however, some time later, he lost his ship in a storm, after which he never regained his former reputation because, to quote Antônio Barata: 'The community could accept indifference to danger or recklessness with tolerance and even admiration as long as there was hope of some rewarding victory and looting. However, nobody had ever benefited from a destructive hurricane, and anyone unmindful of gales was considered insane.' "

Octávio has listened to this old yarn with an amused smile.

"No," he says. "I don't think that this man was a relative of mine ... As far as I know, there's no pirate blood running in our family. And I've never attacked anybody, except perhaps an inspector from the Revenue Department ..." They laugh and the Portuguese goes on: "I've also heard about a certain Captain Birobidjan ..."

Mayer Guinzburg turns red in the face. "Have you? And what have you heard about me? That's all in the past now ..."

"That's true, it's all in the past," murmurs Octávio. They fall silent.

David Benveniste walks in and sits down next to them. "What time is it?" he asks.

"Nine o'clock," replies Mayer.

"Nine o'clock? Is that all? So there's still another three hours before lunch!" mutters Benveniste.

He turns on the battery-operated radio. The newscaster's excited voice invades the living room. It's June 7, the third day of the Six-Day War. Israeli tanks advance in the Sinai. Mayer Guinzburg and David Benveniste listen attentively. When the newscast is over, Benveniste turns off the radio. "Well," he mumbles, "it seems that the matter is settled."

"It would seem so," says Mayer cautiously. He senses that an argument is about to start.

"It serves him right. That Nasser," Benveniste says with irritation. "It's because of him that I'm now in this boarding house when I could be in my office in Cairo ... It serves him right. That demagogue. He'll pay for it."

"However," Mayer reasons, "he's a man of character, a born leader, as even Ben Gurion concedes. He has tried to pull his country out of underdevelopment ..."

"That's true," admits David. "He's a great man. It was really possible for us to get along with him. I still remember his yearly visits to the synagogue around New Year's Day. On one occasion I even had the opportunity to greet him—"

"Yet sooner or later," Mayer interrupts him, "you would have to confront him. After all, he is a dictator. The likes of him are quite unpredictable."

"Maybe," says David Benveniste. "However, the fact is that we did have a good life in Egypt. For centuries, as a matter of fact. Maimonides, for instance, was Sultan Saladin's personal physician ... Yes, we did have a good life there. But you Russian Jews had to create Zionism and Israel. Because you had been harassed by anti-Semitism and suffered through pogroms you felt you had to jeopardize the rest of us as well. We were not involved at all in your situation. We were prospering ..."

"Sure you were," exclaims Mayer, irritated. "While the Egyptian people were living in abysmal poverty you were rolling in money!"

"True," admits Benveniste. "But deep down we were seen as foreigners. And it wasn't easy for us to have to suffer the envy of those people. Sooner or later we would have been forced to leave and go to some other country, to Israel, who knows ..."

"Well," says Mayer in a more conciliatory tone, "if we really get down to the heart of the matter, they had no right to kick you out. Your exploitation of the people was zilch compared to what others were doing ... say, the oil trusts ..."

"But that's precisely what happened!" shouts Benveniste. "An association of ideas! People had this image of the Jews being connected with Israel, and of Israel always siding with the United States, with imperialism!"

"Now, wait a minute!" Mayer raises a finger. "Siding with imperialism? What do you mean, siding with imperialism? The United States and American imperialism are quite distinct from each other! Israel got help from the American Jews, and that's only fair, isn't it? Just as the Italians got help from the Italo-Americans ..."

"That's right. But how can you expect the Egyptians, semiliterate as they are, to distinguish between the two? Besides—what time is it?"

"Ten o'clock," says Octávio.*

"Ten o'clock? Is that all?" groans David Benveniste.† "Another two hours until lunch!"

"It will come," says Mayer. "We can be sure that lunchtime will come and go. The days will come and go, rivers of soup will flow, bowels will empty themselves and will fill up again; in the bathroom, people will squabble, and after coffee, they'll chat; they'll sleep and they'll wake up again; maybe they'll get sick, maybe they'll die.

Sometimes in the evening Mayer Guinzburg will go for a walk along the dew-sodden trails. His shoes will sink into the damp soil; suddenly, he'll find himself no longer walking, but floating, half-drowned, in the dense fog that will slowly carry him forward amid the trunks of scrubby trees. Skulls, afloat, will drift by: Comrade Pig's, Comrade Goat's; scraps of paper will swirl around him, and even without reading he knows what's written on them: "The corn crop will be beyond all expectations ..." He will arrive at the ruins of the Palace of Cul-

---

*Octávio Rodrigues. Later his son would say about him, as he reminisced: "His eyes were as sprightly as two little mice. He had a beautiful mustache. His skin was still sleek—in a seventy-eight-year-old man!"

†David Benveniste. This is how his daughter described him: "His face looked like a rat's snout. He wore a mustache, which always looked dirty. There was a lecherous glitter in his beady eyes—in an eighty-one-year-old man! The shamelessness!" This lady suffered from emotional problems; she went for treatment to Octávio Rodrigues's son, a psychologist, whom she had met during one of her visits to the boarding house.

ture, of the Heroes' Mausoleum; and then the subtle current will carry him back and deposit him carefully, tenderly, at the doorstep of the Sofia Boarding House. He will go in; chilled to the bone. He will go to bed. The sheets will welcome him with a cold embrace; without any resentment, without any selfishness, Mayer will share with them his own meager warmth. And then he will be able to fall asleep.

1970

D URING THAT YEAR THE PORTUGUESE HAD FEW
new stories to tell. David Benveniste's constipation was getting
worse; he was now constantly pounding on the bathroom door,
threatening Mayer with acts of terrorism.

"One of these days I'll put a bomb there, you Russian!"

Ana Souza could no longer feed herself after she suffered a
stroke, which left her paralyzed on her right side. No other
boarders ever moved in.

Swamped with work, Dona Sofia would occasionally enlist the
boarders' help. David Benveniste would refuse to help, saying
that he was not a servant, that he was a paying guest, that he
had worked enough in his life. The Portuguese would go to
the kitchen and cook some salt cod, one of his specialties, while
singing fados, those sorrowful, nostalgic Portuguese songs. As
for Mayer Guinzburg, he would occasionally do the dishes, muttering: "It's disgraceful. A man like me ..." Standing on the
sink, the little men watched him in silence. Once Mayer Guinzburg
filled the sink with water and went to the pantry to get some
scouring powder. When he returned, he saw that three of the

little men had fallen into the water and were floating, motionless. Maybe they're only half-drowned, Mayer said to himself, and
hurried to their rescue. He touched them with his finger: hope-
lessly drowned. With a sigh, he pulled the plug out of the sink.
The tiny creatures began to spin; at first slowly, then increasingly faster, they were sucked into the whirlpool. Then came the
final vortex and they were sucked down the drain and, shriveled as they were, they had no difficulty passing through the
strainer. Mayer Guinzburg closes his eyes and imagines the route
of the tiny corpses: they will descend with the thick black liquid,
which flows purling through the sewage pipe; they'll reach the
vast Guaíba River, where the diminutive corpses will sink to the
bottom; stripped of their flesh, their tiny skulls will show white
and their bones will lie buried forever in the mud and silt of the
estuary. From then on, Mayer Guinzburg refused to help in
the kitchen.

Dona Sofia hired a servant who lived in the neighborhood.
Mayer Guinzburg was surprised to hear that her name was
Santinha. He watched her carefully as she ladled out soup. Something about her reminded him of Rosa Luxemburg; her eyes,
however, weren't blue but brown; her skin was dark ... After
lunch Mayer didn't go to his room; he remained seated in the
dining room, watching Santinha, who was clearing the table.

"Why do people call you Santinha?" he wanted to know.

"Gosh, because it's my name, that's why!" she said, surprised.
"Santa Terezinha da Silva. Santinha is my nickname."

"Are you named after your mother?" Mayer could barely contain his anxiety.

The young woman stared at him in astonishment.

"Of course not. Why should the two of us have the same name?
My mother's name is Aurora."

"And ..." Mayer went on, still hopeful, "and your father? Was
his name Nandinho?"

"Nandinho?" She broke into laughter. "Heavens, no!"

"Was it Hortensio then? Libório maybe? Or Fuinha?"

"Fuinha!" She was now doubled up with laughter. "You're such a funny man, Senhor Mayer. Fuinha! The idea! Of course not!" Mayer was chagrined, but began to laugh with her. "If my father heard you, he'd beat you up. His name is Antão, Senhor Mayer."

They went on laughing together for a while.

"Don't call me 'Senhor,' just 'Mayer,'" he said.

She looked at him with suspicion.

"I can call you Mayer, but Dona Sofia won't like it. She told me to treat everybody here with respect ..."

"Then call me 'Captain.' It's a respectful title!"

"Captain!" She broke into laughter again. "Are you a captain, really?"

"I used to be," said Mayer. Dona Sofia came in. He got up and went to his room.

Mayer Guinzburg knows that he won't be able to sleep that night. He will get up, will walk cautiously through the house, will open the front door, will go outside: In the small wooden room where Santinha sleeps the light is still on; he will knock on the door and go in. "What's the matter, Captain?" she'll ask, with a mixture of fear and amusement. He'll come up with an excuse—but what kind of excuse? Ah, yes—he's got this pain in his back and needs a massage—and she, laughing, will begin to massage his back gently, and before long the massage will become an embrace ... Lying on top of Santinha, Mayer Guinzburg lets out moans of pain and pleasure. But whenever he's about to come, a terrible pain pierces his chest. He rests for a while and tries again.

"Is something wrong, Captain?" asks Santinha, frightened.

"No, it's nothing. Just wait a moment, will you? Just a moment ..."

The door swings open and a figure looms over them: It's Dona Sofia.

"Get out," she says to Mayer in a cold voice.

Without a word, he picks up his clothes and leaves.

Later, in his room, he feels outraged. "How dare she boss me around like that? It's disgraceful!" That night he didn't get a wink of sleep.

The following morning, while Mayer is still in bed, there is a knock on the door. "Who is it?" he asks, annoyed. "It's me, Sofia. May I come in?"

"Yes."

She opens the door, a conciliatory smile on her face.

"I'd like to apologize, Mayer ... for what happened last night." He doesn't reply. "I realize you must feel lonesome at times."

"That's true," concedes Mayer.

His reply emboldens her to ask: "May I sit down?"

Without waiting for his reply, she sits down on the edge of the bed.

"I've been thinking, Mayer ..." She hesitates. Suddenly, the words come pouring out of her mouth, trampling on one another. "I'll get straight to the point. As you know, I'm an enterprising woman and don't mince any words. What I mean is: You're lonesome, that's why you do foolish things like last night. But I'm lonesome too. I've never married, and we do get sick and tired of living alone. So, if we ... if we agreed, you know, to ... The house could be expanded ..."

"No, Sofia—" Mayer begins.

"It would be good to have a man around," she quickly cuts in. "And if you'd rather, Mayer, we could be just good friends. Sex, well ... I don't care about it; it doesn't interest me, I assure you. As soon as—"

"No, Sofia," Mayer interrupts her. "We'd better not talk about it anymore. It wouldn't work."

"But Mayer—"

"No, it won't work."

She gets to her feet.

"All right, so it won't. And I know why it won't work: It's because of your infatuation with that little hussy, isn't it? Well, let me tell you something. If I'm not giving her the gate, it's because I can't do without a servant. But from now on, it's war between us! A state of declared war, do you hear me, Captain Birobidjan? You old coot!"

In the following days, several changes took place at the Sofia Boarding House. The first of these was a bulletin board in the hall, where two notices were posted: one announcing a new, stricter schedule for meals, and the other announcing that the servant was not allowed to talk to the boarders, except in cases strictly pertaining to the operation of the boarding house.

"What's eating Dona Sofia?" asked the Portuguese, rather surprised. "The old Jewess from the Russian steppes," muttered Benveniste. Sofia, who happened to be walking by, overheard him. That very day another notice went up, reminding the boarders that the bathroom was a common facility and that its use was limited to fifteen minutes per person.

"The hell it is!" shouted Benveniste. "I'm paying, and I'll stay in there for as long as I want!"

Right away he went to the bathroom and closed the door. Dona Sofia told Santinha to keep knocking on the door until he came out—which she did, feeling uncomfortable and breaking into fits of giggling. David Benveniste endured this situation for fifteen minutes; then he came out and shut himself up in his room. He refused to have lunch.

Meanwhile, the quality of the meals was deteriorating. The Portuguese thought that Dona Sofia must be going through difficulties—perhaps of a financial nature—or having problems with the maid. But he didn't dare ask her. Once he asked Santinha if he could help her, and he was in the kitchen cooking some dried cod when Dona Sofia came in.

131

"I was lending her a hand ..." the Portuguese explained sheepishly.

Dona Sofia didn't say anything. However, later that day there was a new notice on the bulletin board saying that boarders were not allowed in the kitchen.

Mayer was feeling depressed. He would spend the whole day in his room, lying in bed and staring at the ceiling. He was having chest pains; he knew he should see Dr. Finkelstein, but was the old doctor of Bom Fim still alive? Anyhow, he didn't have any money; Jorge paid for his board and room, but he hadn't shown up at the boarding house in a long time.

"Your son has probably been too busy," the Portuguese said, trying to comfort him. "And this place is quite far ..."

"Far, my foot! Beco do Salso has become another district of the city, it's not like in the old days at all ..."

At times he felt like telling his friend about New Birobidjan, but he seemed unable to whip up enough enthusiasm to do so. How could one talk to a Gentile about the Jewish anguish? How could one talk to a former grain merchant about Trotsky, Isaac Babel, and Birobidjan? How could one talk to an old man about building a new society? No, he'd rather remain silent. He'd rather remain silent and pray. Mayer Guinzburg would go to his room, put on the tallith and pray. He prayed and prayed. Standing on the chest of drawers, the little men watched him in silence. Mayer knew that they were waiting for a speech: "All forms of oppression must be eliminated!" It was, however, impossible for him to heed to their request, he had no energy left; he would rather pray.

Then, two things happened.

The first was the arrival of some Russian technicians in Porto Alegre. They were members of a delegation, apparently of no consequence; however, their visit caused quite a stir because as they were leaving the airport, a group of Jews that had been waiting at the entrance, began shouting: "Let my people go!" The press reported the incident with banner headlines and pictures. Reading the newspaper, Mayer was filled with emotion: It seemed to him that one of the young women in the picture was Raquel. "Yes, I'm sure it is. It's my daughter Raquel. Like her father, there she is, right at the front line. The affair with that right-winger Colomy had been nothing but a dream!"

He laughed and laughed, showing the newspaper to David Benveniste, who was watching him in puzzlement. That day, for the first time in many years, Mayer got out his album and made a drawing. It depicts Raquel in front of the Kremlin. With one of her hands, she signals to a group of frightened Jews to follow her; with the other hand she holds the Russian tanks back. Her face glows. Her hands, in particular, look impressive—big and strong. He pinned the drawing over his bed, despite the notice on the bulletin board: "No pictures are allowed on the walls."

This event was followed by another, which later became known as the Day of the Mouse. It began on a cold, rainy morning. It is ten o'clock and Mayer and the Portuguese are sitting on the couch; Ana is in her bedroom, and David Benveniste in the bathroom. All of a sudden, they hear an awful racket in the kitchen: Dishes crash, furniture is overturned. Mayer and the Portuguese rush to the scene, where they find Dona Sofia standing on the table, her toes sunk into the dough she was kneading for lunch.

"Do something!" she hollers, terror-stricken.

The two men are baffled. They can't figure out the reason for her fear. Then she will let out a frightful scream. The windowpanes will resound with the piercing sound; the stucco will fall off the walls, the light bulb will blow out. And in the gray morning light, Mayer will see a mouse lying dead on the stove. They will bend over the small corpse and examine it; they will find no signs of violence. "How odd," they will say.

133

"I've killed the creature with my screams," Dona Sofia will say proudly.*

Octávio will believe her. "With a woman like her, nothing is impossible." Mayer, however, will believe that the mouse was already dead when she started screaming. "There was really no reason at all for her to be frightened."

Dona Sofia will tell Santinha to throw the tiny carcass into the fields. The sun and the rain and the worms and the fermentation will work on it until the skin rots, the flesh comes off, and the tiny white skull is bared.

Mayer Guinzburg capitalizes on this incident. He keeps making remarks. "My friend," he says to Octávio, "if she's afraid of mice, she can't be unconquerable!" Mayer Guinzburg is crafty. He knows how to undermine a landlady's authority. He says to David Benveniste, looking quite concerned: "This constipation of yours will be the death of you ..."

His subversive campaigning pays off. A week later, rebellion breaks out.

The menu had become quite predictable: soup, pasta, a piece of meat—which was invariably tough. "As Sofia grows older, the steak gets tougher," mutters Octávio. Even Mayer Guinzburg, who has good teeth, finds it hard to chew the meat. David Benveniste keeps chewing with his smooth gums, but unsuccessfully. Ana Souza refuses to eat the food that Santinha feeds her.

"She says the meat is too tough, Dona Sofia," Santinha explains.

"Shut up and go back to the kitchen," orders Sofia. She sits down next to Ana, picking up the fork: "Eat."

"I can't, I can't chew this meat ..."

"Eat. The food is good."

---

*About this matter, the National Wildlife Association of the United States has the following explanation: "During the winter, animals lose strength and weight. They can easily die from shock. Disturbing their peace and quiet, or making them run, can put too much stress on their vital systems."

"I can't, I can't!" screams Ana.

Sofia tries to insert a piece of meat into her mouth. Stubbornly, Ana clenches her jaws.

"Eat!"

Mayer Guinzburg gets to his feet. (Later, this scene will be depicted in a drawing: on his face, an expression of justified anger.) "Sofia!"

She goes on fighting with Ana.

"Sofia! Leave the woman alone, will you? Can't you see she doesn't want it? The meat is tough."

The owner of the boarding house puts the fork down on the plate. She gets up and slowly draws closer to Mayer. Then she begins to speak in a low, threatening voice: "Call me 'dona' when you speak to me, Dona Sofia. Do you get it? This afternoon I'll put up a notice regarding this matter, but let me make this very clear right now. Secondly, the meat is excellent. It's grade A and not even the best restaurants—"

"The meat is awful," says Mayer.

"Captain Birobidjan!" yells Sofia, furious. "I know you, you old anarchist! But let me tell you once and for all, I'm the boss around here, understand? And I'll put an end to these shenanigans of yours. To set an example, you're going to eat this meat."

"Sofia, you old bitch," says Mayer with a vicious grin, "you're dead wrong if you think I'm going to eat this tough piece of dewlap that you insist on calling meat."

"Captain, if you don't eat it," replies Sofia, grinning at first and then speaking between her teeth, "I'll beat you to a pulp."

"No, Sofia, you're wrong again. I'm the one who will beat you to a pulp."

"No, you aren't, just wait and see. I'll yank this head of yours out of your body."

"And I'll strip the flesh off your head and expose your skull, you hag!"

A moment later they are scuffling. They fall down, roll under the table, disappear behind the checkered tablecloth. The Portuguese and David Benveniste take refuge in a corner. From under the table some screams and moans. Then there is silence and finally, Mayer's head pops out: "A rope!"

"Right away, Captain!" Octávio rushes to the pantry and is back in a jiffy with a coil of rope. Mayer disappears again under the table, reappearing moments later: "She's all tied up now."

He is panting; his face is badly scratched. Santinha gets the mercurochrome and some cotton wool and dresses his wounds. Mayer plops down on the couch.

"And now? What are we going to do with her?" asks David Benveniste, frightened. "If we untie her, she'll kill us . . ."

"We'll carry her to Santinha's room," says Mayer.

Transporting Sofia turns out to be a complicated yet amusing task. Everybody pitches in; one holds her by the arms, another by the legs. And they begin to carry her. "Watch out! The table! Slowly now. A bit more to the right!" Mayer feels a stab of pain in his chest, but his main concern at the moment is to cheer them on. Suddenly, Sofia's dress is ripped; they let go of her, and she falls with a thudding sound. Santinha is quick to cover her with a towel. The others burst into laughter: Mayer, Octávio, David Benveniste, and even Ana and Santinha, laugh their heads off. Sofia curses them: "Wait until I free myself . . ." Finally, they succeed in locking her in the servant's room.

That evening they feast on dried cod, prepared by Octávio, on tender steaks cooked by Santinha, who announces proudly: "And there's still much more to come!"

A stream of dishes flows in from the kitchen: assorted salads, pasta, sauces, desserts. Out of a cupboard come several bottles of vintage wine. They drink to victory, to liberation, to long life.

Ana recalls the party her father, an old abolitionist, gave on the day when the abolition of slavery in Brazil was proclaimed.

"Long live the Captain!" shouts Octávio. "Long live Captain Birobidjan!"

"No," Mayer protests, "I'm not a Captain ..."

"Captain! Captain!" David Benveniste and the Portuguese embrace him effusively.

Mayer then feels that now is the right moment to make a speech. He gets to his feet, looks at each of them in turn—at the Portuguese, at David Benveniste, at Ana, at Santinha—and announces in a voice that is calm yet forceful, excited yet firm, soft yet clear: "At this moment we begin the building of a new society." He talks about what New Birobidjan will be like. He describes the corn and bean fields, the shelter for the animals; the site of the future power plant; the Palace of Culture; the flagpole and its flag; the newspaper called *The Voice of New Birobidjan* ...

Octávio and David Benveniste listen to him in utter bafflement; Ana Souza snores loudly. Finally, the Portuguese says, embarrassed: "We'd better go to bed now. But first I'd like to have some tea ... Santinha! Where are you?"

She has disappeared. Octávio gives up the idea of having tea. He looks at Ana: "And who's going to carry her to bed?"

"Let her sleep on the couch," mumbles Mayer in a faded tone of voice.

David Benveniste draws nearer and speaks to Mayer in a low voice. "Dona Sofia has a TV set in her room. Can I have it? After all, everything belongs to us, doesn't it? Will you get it for me, Mayer?"

"You don't understand." Mayer feels like explaining. "That's not it at all—it's got nothing to do with plundering. It's a new society that we're trying to build ..." He stops talking when he sees the beseeching look in the other man's eyes. Heaving a sigh, he enters Sophia's room. He can't find the light switch and all of a sudden he detects a figure lying on the bed. He approaches with caution. It's Santinha. He shakes her: "What do you think you're doing here?"

She sits up, startled; then, recognizing Mayer, she stretches out and laughs: "Everything belongs to us, doesn't it? Well, I've chosen this room for myself. Besides, you've taken Dona Sofia to my room . . ."

"Get out," Mayer commands in a gruff voice.

"Captain . . . Come on, my little Captain, don't be like that . . . Come here, you meany!"

She reaches her arms out. Her teeth glint in the semidarkness. Mayer hesitates; he gulps. Then he locks the door and begins to unbutton his shirt.

"Captain!" Benveniste shouts outside the door. "What about the TV set?"

Santinha holds him in her arms and nibbles at his ear.

"Captain, you old bugger!" Benveniste shouts. "You've shut yourself up so that you can watch TV all by yourself, isn't that so? Open the door, you Jewish thief! You filthy Jew!" Then he walks away grumbling.

A pain clutches Mayer's chest like a talon; rent by pain and orgasm, he breathes heavily; finally, he collapses onto the bed.

"Oh, Captain!" murmurs Santinha, who is both exhausted and surprised. "Oh shit, Captain, I'd never have guessed you could be so good . . ."

She kisses him, turns her back to him, and falls asleep. Mayer lies awake for a long time; when the noises in the house finally die down, he too falls asleep.

On the following day the captain oversleeps. He wakes up annoyed: There is a lengthy program ahead—the election of the members of the Central Committee; a meeting to discuss the five-year plan and the collectivization of all private property . . . And it's already ten o'clock! The captain jumps out of bed, puts on his pants and leaves the room. He runs into the Portuguese, who is suffering from a bout of diarrhea. David Benveniste is already installed in the bathroom, announcing that he has taken permanent possession of the place. The house looks topsy-turvy, the table cluttered with dirty dishes. Lying on the couch, Ana cries with hunger. The captain goes back to Santinha to ask her to make coffee. He finds her asleep. He tries to wake her up, at first with tenderness, which soon changes into a feeling of irritation.

"I'm not working today," she murmurs, heavy-lidded. "It's my day off. And besides, I'm a free woman now. I can sleep as much as I want."

The captain sighs. He realizes they are in a hopeless situation. The milk will turn sour, the bread will become stale, the butter will run—and she won't get up. That's what alienation feels like.

Birobidjan returns to the living room without knowing what to do next. He is thinking of having a people's rally in front of the house, where they will attend the flag raising ceremony.

"I'm hungry!" shouts David Benveniste as he leaves the bathroom. Mayer Guinzburg decides to postpone the rally (one step backward; later, two forward), and to see about putting a meal together. Stoically, he goes to the kitchen, where an unpleasant surprise awaits him: Someone left the water running and the sink has overflowed. The kitchen is flooded. Plates, flatware, and pots and pans lie scattered all over the kitchen.

"Ah, Léia," he moans, collapsing onto a chair. "Ah, Léia." It wasn't a slip of the tongue. It's his wife—the strength of her powerful arms, the courage in her heart—that he now invokes. He takes off his shoes, rolls up the legs of his pants, and gets to his feet. He walks through the dirty water, tidying up the kitchen the best he can. Soon the fire will be ablaze, the water will boil, the bread will be baked, and the coffee will be ready. Birobidjan toils on cheerfully, humming "El Ejército del Ebro." From the doorway, his fellow boarders look on in amazement.

"Come on, join me, comrades! Work has never disgraced anybody."

David Benveniste refuses. Octávio joins him, but he does so reluctantly. As it turns out, he hinders rather than helps Mayer in his work. Octávio takes Sophia's best chinaware out of a cupboard; shaking badly as he is, he breaks several cups. Birobidjan hesitates over the choice between sending him away, thereby incurring the risk of losing a comrade, and praising him, thereby losing more cups. Cups, however, are aplenty, whereas good men are scarce, so he opts for the second choice. He resumes his work while hearing with resignation the chinaware being reduced to pieces: "There are always plastic cups . . ."

Finally, they sit down at the table for breakfast. Birobidjan would like to make a short speech before they eat, but David Benveniste is unwilling to wait and pitches into the food; and so does the Portuguese, who although more restrained, is equally eager to start eating. The captain sets himself the task of waiting on Ana Souza, who has been whimpering nonstop.

"The bread is hard . . . It's too hard . . ."

"It isn't," says the captain. "Eat."

"I don't want to . . ."

"Eat."

Ana Souza then stares at him in surprise: "But who are you?"

"Eat."

With her good hand she throws the plate on the floor. There is a tense moment. Birobidjan finds it hard to control himself.

He picks up the plate, wondering what to do next in order to maintain his authority, without, however, generating any further opposition. Then it occurs to him: Why not dunk the bread in the coffee?

"There! Try it now!"

Somewhat suspiciously, Ana Souza opens her mouth. As she chews, the captain's chest begins to swell with a mixture of feelings: triumphant pride, relief, deep joy. And when the last crumb

140

disappears behind Ana's gums, he lets out a yell of pride: "See? Good, wasn't it?"

Birobidjan and the Portuguese applaud; Ana smiles timidly. Birobidjan decides now is the right time to call a mass rally. He gets to his feet. Santinha appears at the doorway, yawning openly. "Is there any food left?"

Birobidjan stares at her, a stern expression on his face. "People who don't work aren't entitled to eat. That's the cardinal rule of New Birobidjan."

"Of what?" she asks, trying to grab a slice of bread. Birobidjan slaps her on the hand. The Portuguese and Benveniste, frightened, get up.

"What's the matter with you, Captain?" Sentinha asks with irritation. And then in a different tone of voice, "Have you already forgotten about last night?"

"Personal relations should never interfere with productivity relations."

The little men standing on the table break into applause.

"All right," she says, "so you're not letting me have any food, right? Well, let me tell you then that I'm not going to lift a finger to help you in any way."

She returns to her room. Birobidjan sighs and begins to clear away the plates. And it is only then that he remembers Sophia: He'll have to feed her, despite the fact that she is an enemy. As a matter of fact, Birobidjan says to himself, the way she is is not her fault, that's the way she was brought up, and who knows, living in a new society might change her ... He puts some bread, cheese, and a cup of coffee on a tray and carries it to the servant's room, from where come frightful yells: "Let me out of here, you dogs!"

Mayer enters the room.

"Get out of here, Captain," she yells. She has fallen off the bed, and although still all tied up, she has succeeded in making the room look like a battlefield: There are broken knick-knacks all over, and the furniture is overturned.

"I've brought you breakfast, Sofia."

"*Dona* Sofia, do you hear? *Dona* Sofia! And now get out of here! I don't want anything from you. You'll have to answer to the police for this, just wait and see, you thief! You weren't satisfied with pilfering a few odd things here and there, but you had to take the entire boarding house too!"

Birobidjan sits down on the floor, next to her. "Come on, Sofia. Here; I'll feed you."

"No, you won't. Get out of here!"

"Eat," he says, trying to insert some bread into her mouth.

"I don't want to eat." She shakes her head.

"Eat."

She resists for a while, but she's really starving. She finally takes a bite of the bread.

"The bread's hard. When I was running the boarding house the bread was always fresh."

"It still is. And there's no boarding house anymore. This place has been renamed New Birobidjan. We're going to build a new society here. Eat."

"What?!" Sofia opens her eyes wide. "But you're nuts, Mayer! What new society? Are you talking about the old Maykir Club? Maykir is finished. It went bankrupt, don't you remember? At the time they wanted to commit you to a mental hospital; your son opposed the idea. Then he came to see me here. I didn't want to have you as a boarder; I'm poor, Mayer, but I'm a sensible person. I didn't want to get mixed up with a nut case, but he kept insisting and I finally gave in. And now here I am, all tied up. It serves me right. A punishment for having been much too kind."

"You'll have to go through an educational process," Mayer explains, "and then you'll be able to accept the ideas of the new society. Later we'll set you free. There's nothing to be afraid of;

I'm not going to hand you over to the People's Tribunal, which would likely sentence you to death. I think that your problems stem from the way you were brought up; therefore, I'm willing to give you the opportunity to reform. Hard work will regenerate you. But now, eat."

"No! You're a raving lunatic!"

The captain tries to shove a piece of bread into her mouth. Stubbornly, she clenches her teeth. He gives up, and gets to his feet.

"See?" shouts Sofia, triumphant. "See who's stronger? I'll defeat you, Mayer. I'm going on a hunger strike, like the Russian Jews. 'Let my people go.' You've heard about it, haven't you? We'll see which of the two of us will yield first. I'll bet it's not going to be me. I can go without food for a long time. It'll do me good too, for I'm too fat."

Annoyed, Birobidjan leaves the room. He consults his watch: almost eleven o'clock. In a moment they'll be clamoring for lunch. First, however, he has to see to the people's mass rally. He reenters the house and tries to persuade them to step outside. They refuse to do so.

"It's raining," Octávio says in an apologetic tone of voice. It's true: A fine drizzle is falling.

David Benveniste goes to the bathroom; the Portuguese settles himself on the couch.

The captain begins to discourse on work, but nobody shows the slightest interest. He paces the room back and forth; finally, he opens the door and goes out.

He walks past the toolshed and grabs a hoe. He stops at the flagpole; he would like to raise a flag, but there is no flag. For the time being, he is satisfied with hanging a handkerchief on a nail. "Tomorrow there will be a real flag," he murmurs. He is already soaking wet when he says in a loud voice: "At this moment we begin the building of a new society."

He raises the hoe and strikes a blow against the earth. A small

143

groove appears, which soon becomes filled with rainwater. He strikes another blow and the same thing happens. Five minutes later, he feels a sharp pain in his chest. But the captain must not give up now; the Portuguese, Benveniste, and Ana Souza are watching him from one of the windows; he knows they are. He must set an example. He keeps on digging. Then the blade hits something hard.

Birobidjan crouches down and wipes out the mud with his fingers, exposing a whitish object. He digs it up. It is the skull of a pig. Slowly the rain washes away the mud, leaving the bone clean. The captain drops the hoe and returns to the house.

Once again, the atmosphere feels tense: There is no lunch, and Santinha is nowhere to be found.

"I could cook some dried codfish ..." offers the Portuguese. Birobidjan says it's a good idea, then goes to his room and changes into other clothes while he hears dishes crashing in the kitchen.

He is shivering with cold. Suddenly, he is gripped by a pain in his guts. It must be the codfish we had yesterday, he says to himself. He makes a dash for the bathroom: The door is closed.

"Come out, Benveniste!" he shouts, furious. "I must go to the bathroom!"

"You! You!" replies a choked voice. "Who are you?"

Birobidjan is shaking with rage; he steps back and then throws the full weight of his body against the door, which flies open. He lands on Benveniste's lap and the two of them roll on the floor. Birobidjan manages to get to his feet; the other man remains lying on the floor.

"Get up, comrade," says the captain, trying to be conciliatory.

"I can't," whimpers Benveniste. "I'm hurt. And look at what you've done! You pushed me aside just at the very moment when something was beginning to come out! Look, I've dirtied myself!"

Birobidjan offers to help him.

144

"Leave me alone. I'll get up on my own!"

He succeeds in getting to his feet. Moaning, he goes to his room.

Birobidjan goes to the kitchen. The Portuguese is seated in a corner amid a heap of broken china.

"We're out of salted codfish," he says, his voice cracking.

"Never mind. Let's cook something else. You're not letting this get you down, are you? Come on, now, not someone like you, a descendant of pirates. Come on now, cheer up, old chap!"

Octávio laughs. Birobidjan embraces him effusively.

"That's the spirit, comrade! Cheer up! We're building a new society."

He leaves the kitchen in search of the Egyptian; he finds him in his room, grumbling as he packs his belongings.

"Where are you going?"

"To some other boarding house. This one is under the management of a dirty anti-Semite."

"But Comrade Benveniste . . ."

"Excuse me. I have to phone for a cab."

Birobodjan follows him, shouting: "Benveniste! You'll be handed over to the People's Tribunal. You're a reactionary bourgeois!"

"Get lost," replies Benveniste, picking up the phone. Ana looks on in silence.

"You, Portuguese! Come over here!" shouts Birobidjan. "Hurry up, will you? The People's Tribunal will be in session *soon*!"

Octávio comes out of the kitchen, flabbergasted.

"A spoon did you say, Mayer? I can't find any."

"Sit down on the couch next to Ana," orders the captain. And then he makes an announcement: "The People's Tribunal of New Birobidjan is now in session for the first time . . ."

He accuses Benveniste of resorting to Jewish chauvinism to undermine the unity of New Birobidjan.

"Comrades! I demand a stiff sentence!"

At this moment the taxi arrives at the front door, sounding its horn.

"Good-bye, Captain," says Benveniste, and then, turning to the Portuguese, "I'll inform your son about what's been going on, Octávio."

Birobidjan clenches his fists. He feels that they have reached a decisive moment. If David Benveniste goes away, and if he appeals to foreign powers for help, the future of the new society will be in jeopardy. Birobidjan knows that the use of force is justified under such circumstances; right then, however, the taxi driver comes into the room. He used to see Birobidjan at the Serafim.

"How are things with you, Captain? Leading an easy life, nowadays, aren't you? Given up the daily grind, have you, lazybones?" Grinning, he picks up the suitcases and leaves.

"Watch out for the Russians," Benveniste warns as he leaves the house.

For lunch, they eat what is left over from breakfast. As soon as they finish eating, the telephone begins to ring. Birobidjan answers the phone, regretting the fact that he didn't cut off the phone cord. He should have severed all connections with the outside world.

"It's for you, Portuguese."

Octávio hurries to the phone.

"Hello? Yes, son . . ."

For a long time he remains silent, listening.

"All right, son . . . If you think so . . . Okay. I'll be waiting for you." Then he hangs up. "It was my son," he explains to the captain. "The psychologist. He's been told what's been going on. Benveniste's daughter phoned him."

"So, what did he say?" asks Birobidjan gloomily.

"He was explaining that . . . he says that what we're doing is stupid. He says that I identify this house with my mother, that's why I want to have this house, it's because I used to be very attached to my mother. But he says that what we're doing is sheer nonsense, that we—"

"In other words, you're leaving, is that it?"

"Well, yes ..." The Portuguese sounds embarrassed. "He's picking me up in a little while. And there's something else, Captain. We'll be taking Ana with us. I know her family. I can take her to her relatives ... She's being ill-treated here, Captain. She needs somebody to look after her properly, she can't go hungry ... You understand how it is, don't you?"

Birobidjan gets up. "I must get to work now," he says. "There's an awful lot to be done."

"Well ... good-bye then, Captain Birobidjan."

He holds out his hand, which the captain refuses to shake. The Portuguese sighs.

"Would you like me to inform your children?"

Birobidjan doesn't reply and leaves the house. He walks past the toolshed and picks up the hoe.

As he advances upon the muddy soil, his grief begins to abate. He recaptures his former excitement. Birobidjan visualizes vast fields planted with wheat and beans; he visualizes the flag flying high up on the flagpole, he sees the Palace of Culture. His feet sink into the mud, but he plods on joyfully, singing "El Ejército del Ebro." He stops at the place where the skull of Comrade Pig lies; soon he'll build the Heroes' Mausoleum there. He sets to work.

A car approaches. It stops in front of the house. The Portuguese appears at the door. Two men get out of the car, enter the house and a moment later come out carrying Ana Souza; they put her in the car and depart.

The captain keeps on working. There is a pain in his chest, so he rests for a while, and then picks up the hoe once more.

Night is falling. The mist rises in the field. Birobidjan keeps at his work, panting. He feels that he can't take it anymore; however, he would like to lay out at least one of the vegetable patches. At least one.

"Do you need any help?"

He raises his eyes. A few steps away, he sees four figures en-

147

veloped in the fog. Four men wrapped up in sackcloth. Birobidjan is unable to distinguish their faces, but he has no doubts about who they are.

"So, you're back," he mumbles. "You did come back."

Libório and Nandinho and Hortensio and Fuinha ... So, it's going to be war for real.

Birobidjan makes a quick assessment of the situation. If he wants to, he can confront them right then and there, with the hoe—and possibly the skull of Comrade Pig—as a weapon; but the conditions of the terrain are not to his advantage. It would be better for him to withdraw (one step backward, two forward later on) and entrench himself in the house. He drops the hoe and breaks into a run. The four of them stand laughing at him; they don't chase him; instead, they begin to play soccer, using the skull of Comrade Pig as a ball. Libório and Nandinho play against Hortensio and Fuinha. Libório usually is in full control of the ball; Nandinho is an excellent left-winger. Fuinha is good at holding the ball in a clinch, while Hortensio is good at making passes. After the kickoff, Libório passes to Nandinho, who manages to avert Fuinha and then positions himself as if he were a right-winger. On the site of the future Palace of Culture, Fuinha readies himself for a corner kick, but Hortensio hits him from behind. The game is cut short.

As Birobidjan goes past the servant's room, he notices that the door is wide open, the rope lies thrown on the floor, and Sofia has disappeared.

"The treachery!"

Who could have set her free? Santinha? Benveniste? The Portuguese? The four bums? Or did she manage to set herself free? There is no time now to carry out an investigation, and right now he cannot spend time thinking of how to punish the culprits. Later ...

Birobidjan is panting when he reaches the house. He bolts the front door and collapses on the couch. He is exhausted, his chest hurts bady, but he must not give up. He must declare a state of siege without delay and start making the necessary preparations for the defense.

A hand alights on his shoulder. He leaps to his feet, startled. It's Santinha.

"Did I frighten you, Captain?" She breaks into laughter.

"You! But I thought you'd left, Santinha." Overcome by joy, the captain embraces her. "So you didn't leave me?"

"Of course not! I just left to get some food. You didn't let me have anything to eat, not even a piece of bread ..."

"So, that's the reason, you little scoundrel!" The captain laughs so hard that he chokes; in a fit of coughing, he sits down on the couch. "So, you didn't desert me! And here I was thinking that you had betrayed me. I was even considering that at the People's Tribunal I would pass judgment on you by default."

She sits down on the captain's lap, hugs him and kisses him. He knows what she wants—to make love right then and there on the couch, laughing and laughing, and later rolling on the floor. But there is no time now for this kind of frolic. Outside, the enemy is getting ready for the attack. And he will have to defend New Birobidjan all by himself. He can't count on Santinha, who is sadly lacking in ideological foundation, military training, discipline. If only they had more time ... What a comrade she would become, what a comrade! Like Rosa Luxemburg! However, she still has a long way to go and he no longer has the time to teach her. He disentangles himself from her arms and gets to his feet.

"Go and pack your things. I want you to go back to your father's house."

"But why?" she asks, overcome by surprise and alarm. "What have I done, Captain? Did I do something wrong?"

"No, no." Birobidjan tries to think of an explanation. "It's ... well ... you see, I bought this house, didn't you know? And I sent everybody away. I'm going to live here by myself."

149

"Gee, that's great, Captain!" She claps her hands. "Just the two of us!"

"No, Santinha ... You don't understand. The house is for myself only. See what I mean?"

"So you don't want me anymore?" There is an anxious tone in her voice.

"No, Santinha. It wouldn't work. I'm so much older than you ..."

She breaks into tears. "Won't you let me stay ... as a servant?"

He hugs her. "No, I'd never have you here as a servant. Can't you see? I do like you a lot, Santinha ... Now go away."

She wipes her eyes and walks slowly toward the door.

"Farewell, Rosa Luxemburg," murmurs the captain.

"What?" She turns around.

"Nothing, nothing. Please, go now."

From the window, Birobidjan watches her go into her room and then come out again with an old suitcase. It is seven o'clock; he can't afford to waste any more time: The attack will begin as soon as it gets dark. He climbs onto a chair, and as the little men applaud, he proclaims himself the generalissimo of New Birobidjan, adding: "From now on, all forces are under my direct command!"

He scurries about the house, setting up defense. He bolts doors and windows, turns off lights, sets up barricades with pieces of furniture. In the kitchen, he can count on a veritable arsenal of weapons. If the invaders succeed in breaking in, he'll have the means to defend himself: The large kitchen knife will cut, the fork will pierce, the squeezer will squeeze, the rolling pin will flatten, the blender will blend, the spoon will scoop out. Not to mention the Molotov cocktails ... The captain considers making a gigantic homemade bomb: He'll remove the small propane tank from the stove, being careful not to remove the plastic tube attached to it, and then he will carry the tank up to the attic. When the attackers attempt to break in, he will open the

safety valve, set a match to the flow of gas, and drop the tank
on them. The enemy will be destroyed in the explosion. And
if they are not, they will get badly burned. And if they are not,
at least one of them will get crushed. And even if none of this
happens, the explosion will scare the hell out of them. It will teach
them who they are dealing with—Captain Birobidjan, the par-
tisan, the leader of the Resistance, the generalissimo himself! "*No
pasarán!*" Unfortunately, the captain has to give up this plan—
there is no attic in the house. "It was in our old house, the house
on Rua Felipe Camarão ..."

The telephone begins to ring. With the large knife, the captain severs the cord. He doesn't want to talk to the traitors.
He overturns the large leather couch, improvising a hideout, a
bunker, a lair, into which he crawls with difficulty. And there
he stays, dead still.

Little by little his breathing returns to normal. The captain
goes over the details: Has he taken all the necessary measures?
In case of a siege, is he prepared to hold out? Is he hungry? Are
his bowels and bladder empty? He laughs as he thinks of David Benveniste. Now he can have full use of the bathroom whenever he wants to, day or night; he can sit there with the door
open, without having to block it with his hand or foot; he can
take books there, and why not have a library with the works
of Rosa Luxemburg, Marx, Engels, Isaac Babel, Walt Whitman,
Mayakovsky, García Lorca, Jorge Amado, as well as—and why
not?—the Torah, the Gemara, the Mishnah, Antônio Barata's *The
Pirates' Book*, and many many others. He can walk to the bathroom slowly, even if he feels the urge of nature's call—the lei-
surely walk to the bathroom would add spice to the situation.
And if this near glorification of private property ever gives him
a pang of guilt, he can always establish rules to protect himself
from self-corruption. He will divide the number of hours available for the use of the bathroom (a figure obtained by sub-
tracting the hours needed for rest and meals from 24) by the

number of the former residents of the boarding house: In this way, he will obtain his allotted time: two hours and twelve minutes per day. Very well. Although he now lives alone, he won't spend more than two hours and twelve minutes in the bathroom; he will remain consistent. "Even if I am alone, I am both the leader and the masses." At the most, he will increase his allotted time to two and a half hours; it's a small perk, which he is entitled to because of his high level of political awareness and of his constant position in the front lines; and since he has always stimulated other people into new efforts, why shouldn't he now engage himself in self-stimulation?

The captain nods off. He sees the dense forests of New Birobidjan, and Bom Fim, Rua Felipe Camarão, the King David Edifice, Maykir, Leib Kirschblum, José Goldman, Geórgia ... He should do a few more drawings for his album; he will portray himself at the barricades, standing on his feet, a rifle in his hand, a bloodstained bandage on his forehead, his eyes glittering ...

Suddenly, there are sounds outside: footsteps, muffled voices. Indistinct shapes appear at the window, a mocking eye watches him. He clutches the large knife. "*No pasarán!*" Somebody tries the door handle. Then there are knocks on the door. The captain shivers: Have they captured Rosa Luxemburg? Rhythmically, relentlessly, the knocks persist. In his mind's eye, the captain sees the door beginning to yield; the voices sound louder, the tone more triumphant. The enemy is full of self-confidence.

Pain* lunges at him. It pierces his chest, then fans out in a display of power.

The captain gets to his feet, his eyes wide open. Sounds reach his ear, high-pitched sounds, coming from far away, then gradually drawing closer: a siren?

---

*"What kind of pain was it? Was it continuous or intermittent?" asked one of Birobidjan's nephews, the cardiologist, when he heard that a book had been written about his uncle. "Was an electrocardiogram carried out?" Later he added, "As for that incident at the hospital, rather unlikely, I'd say." And much later he said: "As a matter of fact, if you ask me, well, I don't believe a word in this story."

"It's Sofia, with the police!"

He is besieged. Sofia and the policemen will invade the house by knocking down the front door, and a squadron will come in through the back door. It remains to be seen which party will get hold of him first.

"*No pasarán!*" shouts the captain. Then he realizes that if there is still any hope left, this hope is to be found in the people themselves, in all kinds of people: Sofia, the policemen, Libório, Nandinho, Hortensio, Fuinha, the taxi drivers, the Portuguese, Colomy, the real estate agents—they are the people the captain is addressing when he shouts:

"Comrades! We're about to begin the building ..."

He hesitates, and leans against the couch. The lights are turned on. The captain falls forwards. He plunges into the dark sea.

1970.